STRANGE
BUT
TRUE CRIME

The information contained in this book is based on research and sources believed to be reliable as of the publication date. The author and publisher make no representations or warranties as to the accuracy or completeness of the information and will not be held responsible for any errors or omissions.

Copyright © 2023 Burgerson Publishing All rights reserved.

No part of this book may be reproduced, distributed or transmitted in any form or by any means, including photocopying, recording, or other electric or mechanical methods without, the prior written permission of the publisher, except in the case of quotations embodied in reviews and certain other non-commercial uses permitted by copyright law.

First Edition May 2023

Book cover design by Jason Wagner

Interior by Jason Wagner

ISBN: 9798393206000

Published by Jason Wagner

"When a man is denied the right to live the life he believes in, he has no choice but to become an outlaw."

~Nelson Mandela~

Message from the Author

The world of crime is a fascinating and ever-evolving place. While some criminal cases follow a familiar pattern, others push the boundaries of what we think of as "normal." These strange true crimes capture our attention and imagination, challenging our assumptions and reminding us that the criminal mind is complex and often unpredictable.

This book explores some of the most unusual and intriguing criminal cases from around the world, including unusual heists, mysterious murders, bizarre burglaries, oddball arsons, weird white-collar crimes, eccentric extortion, strange serial killers, peculiar Ponzi schemes, curious con artists, and uncommon cyber crimes. Each case offers a unique perspective on the complexities of the criminal mind, and the lengths to which some people will go to achieve their goals.

The cases in this book are not your typical true crime stories. They are unusual and often bizarre, but they are all based on real events. Some are well-known, such as the Gardner Museum Art Heist, where thieves made off with over $500 million worth of artwork in one of the largest art heists in history. Others, such as the Toilet Paper Heist or the Australian Emu Egg Heist, may not be as well-known but are just as fascinating in their own right.

One of the most intriguing cases in this book is the Black Dahlia murder, a notorious case that has fascinated true crime enthusiasts for decades. The victim, Elizabeth Short, was found mutilated and dismembered in a vacant lot in Los Angeles in 1947. The case remains unsolved to this day, and has inspired countless books, movies, and television shows.

Another case that will captivate readers is the London Millennium Dome Raid, which involved a daring heist on New Year's Eve 1999. The thieves, who had spent months planning the robbery, broke into the Millennium Dome and stole over $4 million in diamonds. Their audacity and planning made this one of the most impressive heists in history, and their capture was equally as dramatic.

But not all of the cases in this book involve violent crime. Some, such as the Banco Central Heist in Brazil, were meticulously planned and executed with military precision. In this case, a group of thieves spent months tunneling through several city blocks to reach the bank's vault. Once inside, they made off with over $70 million in cash, making it one of the largest bank heists in history.

The criminals behind these strange crimes are just as varied as their crimes. Some are masterminds who plan their crimes down to the smallest detail, while others are amateurs who stumbled into a life of crime. Some are driven by greed or desperation, while others are motivated by a desire for revenge or a need for excitement.

Despite their differences, all of the cases in this book are united by their ability to capture our attention and imagination. They challenge our assumptions about what is possible, and remind us that the world of crime is not always what it seems. By exploring these strange true crimes, we can gain a deeper understanding of the complexities of the criminal mind, and the lengths to which some people will go to achieve their goals.

This book delves into some of the most unusual and intriguing criminal cases from around the world, offering a unique perspective on the complexities of the criminal mind. Whether you are a true crime enthusiast or just curious about the stranger side of human nature, this book is sure to captivate and intrigue you.

Contents

Unusual Heists 11

    The Toilet Paper Heist 12

    The Great Canadian Maple Syrup Heist 14

    The Gardner Museum Art Heist 16

    The Antwerp Diamond Heist 18

    The London Millennium Dome Raid 20

    The Banco Central Heist 22

    The Hare Krishna Jewel Heist 24

    The Australian Emu Egg Heist 26

    The Vienna Art Museum Heist 28

    The Islington Tunnel Heist 30

Mysterious Murders 32

    The Black Dahlia Murder 33

    The Axeman of New Orleans 35

    The Hinterkaifeck Murders 37

    The Boy in the Box 39

    The Zodiac Killer 41

    The Chicago Tylenol Murders 43

    The Oklahoma Girl Scout Murders 45

    The JonBenét Ramsey Murder 47

    The Villisca Axe Murders 49

    The O.J. Simpson Murder Trial 51

Bizarre Burglaries 53

    The Naptime Burglar 54

    The Toilet Seat Thief 56

    The Honey Heist 58

    The Cereal Killer 60

    The Cheeseburglar 62

    The Snowman Burglar 64

    The Naked Burglar 66

    The Watermelon Thief 68

    The Golf Club Thief 70

    The Chicken Wing Bandit 72

Oddball Arsons 74

    The Pillow Pyro 75

    The Toilet Paper Torch 77

    The Cat Arsonist 79

    The Birthday Cake Burner 81

    The Gas Station Arsonist 83

    The Fireworks Fiend 85

    The DIY Demolition 87

    The Flame-Thrower Arsonist 89

    The Church Burner 91

    The Hot Sauce Hellion 93

Weird White-Collar Crimes 95

    The Caviar Crook 96

    The Trash-Talking Trader 98

    The Naked Trader 100

    The Wine-Sipping Swindler 102

The Email Impersonator 104
The Library Looters 106
The Credit Card Collector 108
The Imposter CEO Scam 110
The Chocolate Con Artist 112
The Art Forgery Faker 114

Eccentric Extortion 116

The Catnapper 117
The Virtual Kidnapper 119
The Robotic Ransom 121
The Celebrity Blackmailer 123
The Bitcoin Bandit 125
The Cemetery Scammer 127
The Baby Extortionist 129
The Virtual Lover 131
The Artful Extortionist 133
The Psychic Scammer 135

Strange Serial Killers 137

Albert Fish 138
Ted Bundy 140
Ed Gein 142
Dennis Rader 144
Jeffrey Dahmer 146
Andrei Chikatilo 148
John Wayne Gacy 150
Richard Ramirez 152

  Aileen Wuornos 154

  Gary Ridgway 156

Peculiar Ponzi Schemes 158

  Charles Ponzi 159

  The Airplane Scheme 161

  The Rubber Ball Scheme 163

  The Cemetery Scheme 165

  The Coconut Plantation Scheme 167

  The Beanie Baby Scheme 169

  The Water Filtration Scheme 171

  The Olive Oil Scheme 173

  The Debt Elimination Scheme 175

  The Female Empowerment Scheme 177

Curious Con Artists 179

  Frank Abagnale Jr. 180

  Victor Lustig 182

  Maria Anna Mozart 184

  George C. Parker 186

  The Fox Sisters 188

  Eduardo de Valfierno 190

  Rachel Dolezal 192

  Frank Bourassa 194

  Anna Sorokin 196

  Elizabeth Holmes 198

Quirky Cybercriminals 200

The World's Most Famous Hacker 201
segvec 203
The Silk Road 205
Solo 207
BadB 209
The Russian 211
The Hacktivist 213
McAfee 215
Seleznev 217
Iceman 219

Unusual Heists

The Toilet Paper Heist

In the wake of the COVID-19 pandemic, one of the most unexpected and bizarre crimes was the Toilet Paper Heist that took place in Hong Kong in February 2020. The sudden shortage of toilet paper across the world led to widespread panic buying and hoarding, which in turn resulted in a surge of thefts and robberies related to toilet paper.

In Hong Kong, one such robbery took place on February 17, 2020, when three masked men entered a delivery truck and made off with HK$1.5 million (US$193,000) worth of toilet paper. The incident took place in the city's Mong Kok district, which is known for its bustling markets and shops.

The robbery quickly gained widespread attention and was covered extensively by the media, both in Hong Kong and around the world. It sparked outrage and disbelief, with many people expressing shock and disbelief that such a crime could take place over something as mundane as toilet paper.

The police launched an extensive investigation into the robbery, and within days, they had made several arrests. A total of seven people were arrested in connection with the heist, including the three men who had carried out the robbery and four others who had allegedly helped them dispose of the stolen goods.

As the investigation unfolded, it emerged that the robbery had been meticulously planned and executed. The robbers had targeted a delivery truck that was carrying a large consignment of toilet paper, and they had used a stolen van to block the vehicle's path. The men then forced their way into the truck and quickly loaded as many rolls of toilet paper as they could carry.

The stolen toilet paper was later recovered by the police, and the suspects were charged with robbery and other related offenses. The incident became known as the "Great Toilet Paper Heist" and was widely mocked and ridiculed on social media and in the press.

However, the Toilet Paper Heist also highlighted the extent to which the COVID-19 pandemic had affected people's behavior and mental state. The sudden shortage of essential goods, including toilet paper, had led to widespread panic buying and hoarding, which in turn had created a black market for these products.

The Toilet Paper Heist was not an isolated incident. Similar thefts and robberies took place in other parts of the world, including Australia and the United States. In some cases, the perpetrators were caught and charged, while in others, they were never identified.

The Toilet Paper Heist also had wider implications for society as a whole. It highlighted the fragility of global supply chains and the vulnerability of essential goods to sudden shocks and disruptions. It also raised questions about the ethics of panic buying and hoarding, and the role that social media and the press play in exacerbating these behaviors.

In the end, the Toilet Paper Heist was a bizarre and unexpected crime that took place in the midst of a global pandemic. It highlighted the lengths that some people will go to in order to obtain essential goods and the fragility of our modern society. It also served as a reminder that even the most mundane of products can have a significant impact on our lives and behavior.

The Great Canadian Maple Syrup Heist

The Great Canadian Maple Syrup Heist is one of the most unusual and audacious heists in modern history. It took place in 2011 in a small warehouse in Quebec, Canada, where the Federation of Quebec Maple Syrup Producers stored its strategic reserve of maple syrup.

The theft was discovered after an inspector visited the warehouse and found that the syrup levels were lower than expected. After further investigation, it was revealed that thieves had been stealing syrup from the warehouse for several months, replacing the stolen syrup with water to avoid detection.

The stolen syrup amounted to approximately 3,000 tons, with an estimated value of $18 million. It represented a significant portion of the Federation of Quebec Maple Syrup Producers' reserve and threatened to destabilize the maple syrup industry in Canada.

The investigation into the heist was extensive and involved multiple law enforcement agencies in Canada and the United States. The suspects were tracked down through a series of interviews and surveillance footage, as well as tips from the public. The investigation revealed that the stolen syrup was being sold on the black market and smuggled across the border into the United States.

The suspects in the case were ultimately charged with a variety of crimes, including theft, fraud, and trafficking stolen goods. Several of the suspects pleaded guilty and were sentenced to prison terms, while others are still awaiting trial.

The Great Canadian Maple Syrup Heist has become a part of Canadian folklore and has been the subject of numerous books, documentaries, and even a television series. It has also highlighted the importance of maple syrup to the Canadian economy and the lengths that some will go to in order to profit from it.

Maple syrup is a valuable commodity in Canada, where it is considered a national treasure and a source of pride for many Canadians. It is produced primarily in the province of Quebec, which accounts for over 70% of the world's maple syrup supply.

The Federation of Quebec Maple Syrup Producers oversees the industry, setting prices and maintaining a strategic reserve of syrup to ensure a stable supply for the market. The reserve is stored in several warehouses across the province, with security measures in place to protect it from theft.

The Great Canadian Maple Syrup Heist was a major blow to the industry, and the Federation of Quebec Maple Syrup Producers has since increased security measures at its warehouses. It has also implemented a system of traceability, which allows it to track the origin of each barrel of syrup to ensure its authenticity.

The heist has also led to increased awareness of the black market trade in maple syrup, which is a growing problem in Canada. Maple syrup is often stolen and sold on the black market, where it can fetch a high price. The syrup is also smuggled across the border into the United States, where it is sold at a premium.

The Great Canadian Maple Syrup Heist has been called the "perfect crime" by some, due to its unusual nature and the difficulty of tracking down the suspects. It has also been compared to other famous heists, such as the 1978 Lufthansa heist in New York City and the 2003 Antwerp diamond heist in Belgium.

The Great Canadian Maple Syrup Heist is a fascinating and unusual heist that has captured the imagination of Canadians and people around the world. It has highlighted the importance of maple syrup to the Canadian economy and the lengths that some will go to in order to profit from it.

The Gardner Museum Art Heist

The Gardner Museum Art Heist is one of the most famous art heists in history. It took place on March 18, 1990, at the Isabella Stewart Gardner Museum in Boston, Massachusetts, where 13 works of art worth an estimated $500 million were stolen.

The heist was carried out by two men dressed as police officers who gained entry to the museum by claiming to be responding to a disturbance call. Once inside, they overpowered the guards and tied them up, proceeding to steal the artworks.

The stolen pieces included paintings by Rembrandt, Vermeer, Degas, and Manet, among others. The heist was a major blow to the art world, and the stolen pieces have never been recovered.

The investigation into the heist was extensive and involved multiple law enforcement agencies in the United States and abroad. The suspects were tracked down through a series of interviews and surveillance footage, as well as tips from the public. However, despite numerous leads, the stolen pieces have never been found and the case remains unsolved.

Over the years, there have been many theories about who was behind the heist and where the stolen artworks are located. Some believe that the pieces were stolen to order by a wealthy collector, while others believe that they were smuggled abroad and sold on the black market.

The Gardner Museum Art Heist has become a part of popular culture and has been the subject of numerous books, documentaries, and even a podcast. It has also highlighted the vulnerability of museums and the importance of security measures in protecting priceless works of art.

The Gardner Museum, which was founded by Isabella Stewart Gardner in 1903, is known for its unique architecture and eclectic collection of artworks from around the world. The museum has since increased its security measures, including the installation of new surveillance cameras and the hiring of additional security staff.

In 2013, the FBI announced that it had identified the suspects behind the heist, but declined to release their names. The agency also announced a $5 million reward for information leading to the recovery of the stolen artworks.

Despite these efforts, the pieces have yet to be found, and their whereabouts remain a mystery. The Gardner Museum Art Heist has become one of the most enduring unsolved mysteries in the art world, and the stolen pieces remain some of the most sought-after artworks in history.

The heist has also had a lasting impact on the art world, inspiring a renewed focus on security measures and the importance of protecting priceless cultural artifacts. It has also highlighted the need for international cooperation in the fight against art theft and the black market trade in stolen artworks.

The Gardner Museum Art Heist is a fascinating and enduring mystery that has captured the imagination of people around the world. It has highlighted the vulnerability of museums and the importance of security measures in protecting priceless works of art. The heist has also had a lasting impact on the art world, inspiring renewed focus on the issue of art theft and the black market trade in stolen artworks. While the stolen pieces have yet to be found, the search continues, and the hope remains that one day they will be recovered and returned to their rightful place in the Gardner Museum.

The Antwerp Diamond Heist

The Antwerp Diamond Heist, also known as the "heist of the century," took place in Antwerp, Belgium on February 15, 2003. The heist involved a group of highly organized thieves who stole diamonds and other precious jewels worth an estimated $100 million from the Antwerp Diamond Center.

The Antwerp Diamond Center is a highly secure building that houses hundreds of diamond dealers and other related businesses. It is considered to be one of the most secure locations in the world for diamonds and other precious gems. The heist was a carefully planned and executed operation that took months of preparation.

The thieves gained access to the building by posing as diamond merchants and using forged documents to enter the vault. Once inside, they disabled the security system and used thermal lances to break into the vault's safe deposit boxes. The heist lasted for several hours, during which time the thieves stole an estimated 123 out of the 160 safe deposit boxes.

The stolen goods included diamonds, gold, and other precious gems, with some of the diamonds estimated to be worth up to $20 million each. The heist was one of the largest diamond thefts in history and shocked the diamond industry and the world.

The investigation into the heist was extensive and involved law enforcement agencies from around the world. The thieves left few clues, and the investigation was hindered by the fact that the stolen diamonds were likely smuggled out of the country and sold on the black market.

Despite a massive manhunt and numerous arrests, the stolen goods were never recovered. The mastermind behind the heist, Leonardo Notarbartolo, was eventually caught and sentenced to 10 years in prison, but the stolen diamonds remain missing to this day.

The Antwerp Diamond Heist has become a subject of fascination for true crime enthusiasts and has been the inspiration for books, documentaries, and movies. It has also had a lasting impact on the diamond industry, leading to increased security measures and awareness of the risks of diamond theft.

The heist also highlighted the global problem of organized crime and the role of criminal networks in the theft and trafficking of precious gems and other high-value goods. It is believed that the stolen diamonds were likely sold on the black market and could still be in circulation today.

The Antwerp Diamond Heist was a sophisticated and daring operation that remains one of the most audacious diamond heists in history. The theft of diamonds and other precious gems worth an estimated $100 million from the Antwerp Diamond Center shocked the diamond industry and the world. Despite an extensive investigation and numerous arrests, the stolen goods were never recovered, and the thieves remain at large. The heist has had a lasting impact on the diamond industry and has highlighted the global problem of organized crime and the trafficking of high-value goods.

The London Millennium Dome Raid

The London Millennium Dome Raid, also known as the Millennium Dome Heist, was a daring robbery that took place on November 7, 2000. The heist was one of the most audacious in British history and involved a group of criminals who attempted to steal over £200 million in diamonds and jewelry from the De Beers diamond exhibit at the Millennium Dome.

The Millennium Dome, located in London's Greenwich Peninsula, was built to celebrate the turn of the millennium and showcase British achievements in science, technology, and culture. The De Beers diamond exhibit was one of the most popular attractions at the Dome, and it featured some of the world's most valuable and rare diamonds, including the Millennium Star, a flawless 203-carat diamond worth an estimated £200 million.

On the day of the heist, a group of six men dressed as security guards arrived at the Dome in a white truck. They claimed to be making a routine pick-up of diamonds from the De Beers exhibit and were allowed to enter the Dome without suspicion. Once inside, the men used a JCB digger to smash through the reinforced glass of the De Beers exhibit and stole several display cases containing diamonds and jewelry.

Despite the robbers' efforts to escape, they were soon intercepted by the police and engaged in a high-speed car chase. The robbers eventually abandoned their getaway car and fled on foot, leaving behind the stolen diamonds and jewelry.

The Millennium Dome Raid was a major embarrassment for the British government, which had invested over £800 million in the construction of the Dome. The robbery exposed major security flaws at the Dome, and it was seen as a sign of the growing sophistication and audacity of criminal gangs in the UK.

In the aftermath of the heist, the police launched a massive manhunt to capture the robbers. Four of the six men involved in the raid were eventually caught and sentenced to a combined total of over 100 years in prison. The two remaining suspects were never apprehended, and their whereabouts remain unknown.

The Millennium Dome Raid had significant cultural and historical implications for the UK. It marked a turning point in the public perception of security and policing, as it highlighted the vulnerabilities of even the most secure locations. It also demonstrated the increasing use of high-tech tools and methods by criminal gangs, as the robbers used a JCB digger to break into the De Beers exhibit.

The heist also had a significant impact on the De Beers diamond company, which suffered a blow to its reputation and image as a result of the robbery. The company was criticized for its lax security measures and for the fact that the diamonds and jewelry stolen from the exhibit had not been insured.

The Millennium Dome Raid remains one of the most daring and audacious robberies in British history. It captured the public imagination and spawned numerous books, documentaries, and films. The heist highlighted the growing sophistication of criminal gangs in the UK and demonstrated the need for increased security measures and policing.

The Millennium Dome Raid was a daring robbery that took place on November 7, 2000, at the De Beers diamond exhibit at the London Millennium Dome. The heist involved a group of six men who used a JCB digger to smash through the reinforced glass of the exhibit and steal several display cases containing diamonds and jewelry. The robbery exposed major security flaws at the Dome and had significant cultural and historical implications for the UK.

The Banco Central Heist

The Banco Central Heist, also known as the Fortaleza Bank Robbery, was a massive bank heist that took place in Fortaleza, Brazil, in 2005. The robbery was one of the largest in history, with the criminals making off with an estimated $70 million in cash.

The Banco Central was the central bank of Brazil, and it stored vast amounts of money in its vaults. The robbers spent months planning the heist and studying the layout of the bank. They rented a nearby commercial property and used it to tunnel underground to the bank's vaults.

The robbers broke into the vaults over a weekend and made off with five large boxes filled with cash. The boxes were so heavy that the robbers had to use a forklift to load them into a stolen truck.

The heist was not discovered until Monday morning when bank employees returned to work. The robbers had left behind a large hole in the bank's wall and a tunnel that led to the commercial property next door.

The Banco Central Heist was a massive blow to the Brazilian government, which had invested heavily in the bank's security measures. The heist exposed major flaws in the bank's security and highlighted the growing sophistication of criminal gangs in Brazil.

The police launched a massive investigation into the heist, but it took them over a year to track down the culprits. The robbers had left few clues behind, but the police eventually arrested a group of suspects who had been living a lavish lifestyle in Fortaleza.

The robbers had used some of the stolen cash to buy expensive cars, yachts, and property. The police were able to track down some of these assets and recover a portion of the stolen cash.

The Banco Central Heist was a complex and audacious robbery that involved months of planning and preparation. The robbers had to overcome numerous obstacles, including the bank's sophisticated security measures and the logistics of moving such a large amount of cash.

The heist also had significant cultural and historical implications for Brazil. It highlighted the growing problem of organized crime in the country and demonstrated the need for increased security measures and policing.

The Banco Central Heist is still considered one of the most audacious bank robberies in history. It inspired numerous books, documentaries, and films and continues to capture the public imagination to this day.

The Banco Central Heist was a massive bank robbery that took place in Fortaleza, Brazil, in 2005. The robbers spent months planning the heist and tunneled underground to the bank's vaults. They made off with an estimated $70 million in cash, making it one of the largest bank robberies in history. The heist exposed major flaws in the bank's security and highlighted the growing problem of organized crime in Brazil. The police eventually arrested a group of suspects and recovered a portion of the stolen cash. The Banco Central Heist remains one of the most audacious bank robberies in history and continues to capture the public imagination to this day.

The Hare Krishna Jewel Heist

The Hare Krishna Jewel Heist was a daring robbery that took place in 1977 in London, England. The robbery was carried out by a group of Hare Krishna devotees, who had turned to crime in order to fund their religious activities.

The Hare Krishna movement, also known as the International Society for Krishna Consciousness (ISKCON), is a religious organization that originated in India in the 1960s. The movement advocates devotion to the Hindu god Krishna and promotes vegetarianism, meditation, and spiritual enlightenment.

The Hare Krishna Jewel Heist began when a group of devotees decided to rob the high-end jeweler, Graff Diamonds, located in London's Mayfair district. The group had been inspired by a previous robbery carried out by the Pink Panthers, a group of Balkan criminals who had stolen millions of dollars worth of jewels from the same store.

The Hare Krishnas spent months planning the heist, studying the layout of the store and its security measures. They also practiced meditation and visualization techniques to help them remain calm and focused during the robbery.

On August 28, 1977, the group of five Hare Krishnas entered the Graff Diamonds store wearing suits, ties, and fedoras. They presented themselves as wealthy customers and asked to see the store's most expensive jewels.

Once they were shown the jewels, the Hare Krishnas drew pistols and threatened the store's employees. They then proceeded to smash the display cases with hammers and grabbed as much jewelry as they could carry. They made off with an estimated £1.5 million worth of jewels, including diamonds, emeralds, and rubies.

The Hare Krishnas escaped on foot, leaving behind a trail of broken glass and terrified employees. They split up and fled in different directions, making it difficult for the police to track them down.

The Hare Krishna Jewel Heist was a major embarrassment for the British police, who were criticized for their slow response to the robbery. The Hare Krishnas had planned the heist meticulously, and they had managed to evade the police for months after the robbery.

The police eventually caught up with the Hare Krishnas when they attempted to sell the stolen jewels in Amsterdam. One of the robbers, Baldeva Prasad, was arrested at the airport with a bag containing £10,000 in cash and several stolen diamonds. The other members of the group were arrested shortly afterward.

The Hare Krishna Jewel Heist was a shocking crime that surprised many people, especially those who knew the Hare Krishnas as a peaceful and religious group. The robbery was also significant because it highlighted the growing problem of cults and religious groups turning to crime in order to fund their activities.

The Hare Krishna Jewel Heist also inspired numerous books, documentaries, and films. The most famous of these is the film "The Great British Train Robbery," which is based on the Hare Krishna Jewel Heist and other major robberies carried out in the UK during the 1960s and 1970s.

The Hare Krishna Jewel Heist was a daring and audacious robbery carried out by a group of Hare Krishna devotees in London in 1977. The robbery was meticulously planned and executed, and the Hare Krishnas managed to make off with £1.5 million worth of jewels. The robbery was a major embarrassment for the British police, who were criticized for their slow response to the crime.

The Australian Emu Egg Heist

The Australian Emu Egg Heist was a daring crime that took place in 2018, in the town of Quirindi, in New South Wales, Australia. The heist involved the theft of several rare and valuable emu eggs from a local farm. The eggs were reportedly worth more than $10,000 and were highly prized by collectors and enthusiasts all over the world.

Emu eggs are large and beautiful, with a distinctive greenish-blue color and a unique pattern of spots and speckles. They are prized by collectors and artists for their aesthetic value and are also used in traditional Aboriginal art and medicine.

The emu is a protected species in Australia, and it is illegal to hunt or trade in emu eggs without a license. The eggs are also subject to strict export controls, and anyone caught trying to smuggle them out of the country can face heavy fines and even imprisonment.

The Australian Emu Egg Heist began when a group of thieves broke into a local farm and stole several emu eggs that were being kept in an incubator. The thieves were reportedly very careful and methodical, taking care not to damage the eggs or disturb the surrounding environment.

The owners of the farm were devastated by the loss of the eggs, which they had been carefully nurturing for months. They immediately reported the theft to the police, who launched a major investigation to try and track down the culprits.

The police were able to obtain CCTV footage of the thieves, which showed them using cutting tools to break into the farm and steal the eggs. They were also able to identify the vehicle that the thieves used to transport the eggs away from the scene of the crime.

Using this information, the police were able to track down the thieves and recover most of the stolen eggs. The thieves were arrested and charged with a range of offenses, including theft, property damage, and the illegal possession of protected wildlife.

The Australian Emu Egg Heist was a shocking crime that attracted widespread attention both in Australia and around the world. The theft of the eggs was seen as a serious blow to the conservation efforts that were being made to protect the emu, which is an iconic and endangered species in Australia.

The heist also highlighted the growing problem of wildlife trafficking, which is a major issue in many parts of the world. Criminal gangs and individuals are known to smuggle rare and endangered species out of countries in order to sell them on the black market, where they can fetch high prices.

The Australian government has taken a strong stance against wildlife trafficking and has introduced a range of measures to try and prevent it from happening. These include increased surveillance and policing of wildlife trade, tougher penalties for offenders, and greater cooperation with international agencies to crack down on the trade.

Despite these efforts, however, wildlife trafficking remains a major problem in many parts of the world. The demand for rare and exotic species continues to fuel a lucrative trade in wildlife, which is estimated to be worth billions of dollars each year.

The Australian Emu Egg Heist was a reminder of the need to protect and preserve our natural heritage, and to take a strong stance against those who would seek to profit from its destruction. The emu is an iconic and beloved symbol of Australia, and it is up to all of us to ensure that it is protected for future generations to enjoy.

The Vienna Art Museum Heist

The Vienna Art Museum Heist, also known as the Kunsthistorisches Museum theft, occurred on November 11, 2003, when thieves broke into the museum and stole several valuable artworks. The Kunsthistorisches Museum, located in Vienna, Austria, is one of the most important art museums in the world, featuring works by famous artists such as Caravaggio, Raphael, and Vermeer.

The heist was carried out by three thieves who managed to enter the museum by climbing a scaffold and breaking a window. Once inside, they quickly made their way to the museum's Coin Cabinet, which contains a collection of rare coins and medals. The thieves used a hydraulic drill to break through the reinforced glass display case, and they made off with approximately 800 coins and medals, worth an estimated €4.5 million.

However, the thieves' main target was the Cellini Salt Cellar, a gold and ivory sculpture created by the famous Italian artist Benvenuto Cellini in the 16th century. The salt cellar is one of the most valuable pieces in the museum's collection, and it is estimated to be worth over €50 million.

The thieves had planned the heist carefully, and they knew exactly where to find the salt cellar. They used an ax to break through the security glass surrounding the display case and quickly made off with the sculpture.

The heist was discovered the following morning when museum staff arrived for work and found the broken display cases. The police were immediately notified, and a major investigation was launched to try and track down the culprits.

The Vienna Art Museum Heist was one of the most audacious art heists of the 21st century, and it shocked the art world. The Cellini Salt Cellar is one of the most valuable and iconic pieces of art in the world, and its theft was a major blow to the museum and to the wider art community.

The investigation into the heist was complex and involved multiple agencies, including Interpol and the FBI. The police quickly identified the thieves as members of a criminal gang from the former Yugoslavia, and they were able to track down the gang's leader, Robert Mang, who was living in Serbia.

Mang was arrested and extradited to Austria, where he was tried and sentenced to ten years in prison for his role in the heist. However, the Cellini Salt Cellar remained missing, and the police were unable to recover it.

The search for the missing salt cellar continued for several years, with the police following up on leads and investigating possible sightings of the sculpture. Finally, in 2006, the salt cellar was discovered buried in a forest near Vienna.

The recovery of the Cellini Salt Cellar was a major triumph for the police and the museum, and it was a relief to the art community, who feared that the priceless artwork had been lost forever. The salt cellar was returned to the museum, where it was restored and put back on display.

The Vienna Art Museum Heist was a reminder of the need to protect and preserve our cultural heritage. The theft of valuable artworks is a serious crime, and it is important for museums and other cultural institutions to have strong security measures in place to prevent such incidents from happening.

The heist also highlighted the growing problem of art theft and trafficking, which is a major issue in many parts of the world. Criminal gangs and individuals are known to steal valuable artworks and sell them on the black market, where they can fetch high prices.

The Islington Tunnel Heist

The Islington Tunnel Heist, also known as the Great Northern Railway Robbery, took place in London, England in 1854. It was one of the most audacious railway heists of the Victorian era, and it captured the imagination of the public and the press.

The Islington Tunnel was part of the Great Northern Railway, which was one of the major railway networks in England at the time. The tunnel was located in north London and was used to transport goods and materials from one end of the city to the other.

The heist was carried out by a group of professional thieves who had been planning the robbery for several months. They knew that a train carrying a large shipment of gold bullion was due to pass through the Islington Tunnel, and they saw an opportunity to make a fortune.

The gang's plan was simple but daring. They would wait at the entrance to the tunnel and derail the train by removing a section of the track. Once the train had come to a halt, they would use explosives to blow open the door of the bullion van and steal the gold.

On the night of the heist, the gang put their plan into action. They waited at the entrance to the tunnel, and when the train approached, they removed the section of track, causing the train to derail. The driver and the guard were overpowered, and the gang used explosives to blow open the door of the bullion van.

However, things did not go according to plan. The explosion caused a large fire, which quickly spread to other parts of the train. The gang panicked and fled the scene, leaving behind the burning train and the stolen gold.

The police were quickly alerted, and they launched a major investigation to try and track down the culprits. They arrested several suspects, but none of them were linked to the heist.

The Islington Tunnel Heist was a major embarrassment for the police and the railway company, and it sparked a public outcry. The press accused the police of incompetence and criticized the railway company for not providing adequate security measures to protect the gold shipment.

The heist also had wider implications for the railway industry. It highlighted the need for better security measures to protect valuable shipments, and it led to the development of new technologies and methods to safeguard railway assets.

The Islington Tunnel Heist remains one of the most famous railway heists in history, and it continues to capture the imagination of people around the world. It has been the subject of numerous books, films, and documentaries, and it has inspired countless works of fiction.

The heist also serves as a cautionary tale about the dangers of greed and the risks involved in criminal activities. The gang in the Islington Tunnel Heist may have thought that they were on the verge of making a fortune, but their actions ultimately led to their downfall.

The Islington Tunnel Heist was a daring and audacious railway robbery that captivated the public and the press. It was a reminder of the need for better security measures to protect valuable assets, and it sparked a wider debate about the role of the police and the railway industry in preventing crime. Today, the Islington Tunnel Heist remains an iconic moment in the history of crime and punishment, and it continues to fascinate and intrigue people around the world.

Mysterious Murders

The Black Dahlia Murder

The Black Dahlia Murder is one of the most notorious and mysterious murders in American history. It involves the brutal and gruesome death of Elizabeth Short, a young woman who was found mutilated and severed in half in a vacant lot in Los Angeles in 1947.

Elizabeth Short was born on July 29, 1924, in Boston, Massachusetts. She grew up in a troubled household and moved to California in her late teens to pursue a career in modeling and acting. However, her dreams never came to fruition, and she struggled to make ends meet.

On January 9, 1947, Elizabeth's body was discovered in a vacant lot in the Leimert Park neighborhood of Los Angeles. Her body was severed in half, and her internal organs had been removed. Her face had been slashed from the corners of her mouth to her ears, giving her a grotesque and disturbing appearance. The killer had also posed her body, spreading her arms and legs apart, in what was later described as a "taunting and grotesque pose."

The investigation into Elizabeth Short's murder quickly became one of the most high-profile cases in Los Angeles history. The media dubbed her "The Black Dahlia," a nickname that referred to her dark hair and the film noir movie that was popular at the time. The case captivated the public, and many people became obsessed with finding the killer.

Despite a massive investigation and the involvement of some of the most skilled detectives in Los Angeles, the killer was never identified. Over the years, dozens of suspects have been considered, including doctors, wealthy businessmen, and even some of Elizabeth's acquaintances. However, no one has ever been charged with the crime, and the case remains unsolved to this day.

One of the most intriguing aspects of the Black Dahlia Murder is the killer's motivation. Some theories suggest that the killer was a deranged doctor or surgeon who wanted to experiment on a human body. Others suggest that the killer was a serial killer who was responsible for other murders in the area. However, there is no concrete evidence to support any of these theories, and the case remains a mystery.

Despite the lack of progress in the investigation, the Black Dahlia Murder has left a lasting impact on American culture. It has been the subject of numerous books, movies, and television shows, and has inspired countless works of art and literature. The murder has become an enduring symbol of the darker side of Los Angeles, and has captured the imaginations of people around the world.

In recent years, there have been some new developments in the case, including the discovery of a potential suspect named George Hodel. Hodel was a wealthy doctor who lived in Los Angeles at the time of the murder and was known to be involved in some of the city's darker subcultures. Some investigators believe that Hodel may have been responsible for the Black Dahlia Murder and other unsolved crimes in the area. However, there is no concrete evidence to support this theory, and the case remains officially unsolved.

The Black Dahlia Murder is a haunting and disturbing case that has captured the imaginations of people around the world for decades. Elizabeth Short's gruesome death and the mystery surrounding her killer have inspired countless works of art and literature, and have become an enduring symbol of the darker side of Los Angeles. Despite decades of investigation and speculation, the killer's identity remains a mystery, and the case continues to fascinate and intrigue people around the world.

The Axeman of New Orleans

The Axeman of New Orleans is one of the most notorious and enigmatic serial killers in American history. The Axeman, whose real identity remains unknown, terrorized New Orleans from 1918 to 1919, murdering at least six people and injuring six more. His modus operandi was always the same: he would break into the homes of his victims in the dead of night, attack them with an axe or a straight razor, and then vanish without a trace.

The Axeman's reign of terror began on May 23, 1918, when he attacked an Italian immigrant named Joseph Maggio and his wife Catherine in their home. The Maggios were found by their neighbors, who heard their screams and rushed to their aid. Catherine was dead, and Joseph died in the hospital the following day. The police found no evidence at the scene, and the investigation soon hit a dead end.

A month later, on June 27, the Axeman struck again. This time, his victim was a grocer named Louis Besumer, who was attacked in his bedroom while he slept. Besumer's wife awakened to find the Axeman standing over her husband's body, brandishing his bloody axe. She screamed, and the Axeman fled, leaving no clues behind.

Over the next several months, the Axeman continued to strike with impunity, seemingly at random. His victims ranged from Italian immigrants to African Americans, from the wealthy to the working-class. The only thing that seemed to connect them was their location: all of the attacks took place in New Orleans or its suburbs.

The Axeman's most famous letter was sent on March 13, 1919, to the New Orleans Times-Picayune. In it, he claimed to be a demon from Hell who spared the lives of those who played jazz music in their homes on the night of March 19. He threatened to kill anyone who did not comply, writing, "If you don't play jazz, you're going to get the axe."

The night of March 19 became known as "The Night of the Axeman," as people throughout New Orleans gathered in homes and bars to play jazz music in an attempt to ward off the killer. As far as anyone knows, the Axeman did not strike that night, but he continued to elude capture for several more months.

The Axeman's last known murder took place on October 27, 1919. His victim was a grocer named Mike Pepitone, who was attacked in his home while his wife and children slept. Pepitone died of his injuries the next day. The police found a bloody axe at the scene, but the Axeman had vanished once again.

Despite a massive manhunt and numerous suspects, the Axeman was never caught. His identity remains a mystery to this day. The case remains one of the most baffling and terrifying unsolved mysteries in American history.

The story of the Axeman of New Orleans has captivated true crime enthusiasts for over a century. The killer's bizarre letters, his strange fixation on jazz music, and his seemingly random choice of victims have all contributed to the legend of the Axeman. Some have even speculated that the Axeman was a member of a secret society or a cult, or that he was a supernatural being with otherworldly powers.

Regardless of the truth behind the legend, the Axeman of New Orleans is a reminder of the power of fear and the mystery of the unknown. His story continues to intrigue and terrify people to this day, and serves as a cautionary tale about the dangers that lurk in the shadows of even the most seemingly peaceful communities.

The Hinterkaifeck Murders

The Hinterkaifeck murders are one of the most perplexing and mysterious cases of murder in German history. The murders were committed in the small farming community of Hinterkaifeck, Bavaria, Germany, in 1922. Six members of the Gruber family were brutally murdered in their home, and the killer was never identified or caught.

The Gruber family consisted of Andreas Gruber, his wife Cäzilia, their daughter Viktoria, her children Cäzilia and Josef, and their maid Maria Baumgartner. They lived on a small farm in a secluded area, with no close neighbors.

On the evening of March 31, 1922, Andreas Gruber went to the nearby town to run some errands, while his wife and daughter stayed at home with the children and the maid. When Andreas returned home, he noticed that someone had tampered with the lock on the front door. He also found that the house was in disarray and that the barn door was open.

Andreas searched the house and discovered the bodies of his wife, daughter, granddaughter, and the maid, all brutally murdered. His grandson, Josef, was missing. Andreas immediately alerted the authorities, and an investigation was launched.

The investigation was hampered by the fact that the crime scene had been disturbed by curious locals before the authorities arrived. However, what was discovered was truly shocking. The maid, Maria Baumgartner, was found dead in her bed, with no visible signs of a struggle. The bodies of Andreas Gruber, his wife Cäzilia, and their daughter Viktoria were found in the barn, beaten to death with a pickaxe. The bodies of their granddaughter, Cäzilia, and her mother, Viktoria, were found in the house, both having been strangled to death.

The most chilling aspect of the crime was that the murderer had stayed in the house for several days after the murders. The family's livestock had been fed and tended to, and meals had been prepared in the kitchen. Neighbors had also reported seeing smoke coming from the chimney, indicating that the killer had stayed in the house and possibly even slept in one of the beds.

Despite an extensive investigation and a nationwide manhunt, the killer was never identified or caught. The Hinterkaifeck murders remain one of Germany's most perplexing unsolved mysteries.

The Hinterkaifeck murders have captured the imagination of true crime enthusiasts and armchair detectives for nearly a century. The brutality of the murders and the fact that the killer remained in the house for several days after the crime make this case truly unique and disturbing.

Over the years, many theories have emerged as to who the killer might have been. Some speculate that it was a jealous lover or a vengeful former employee, while others believe that it was the work of a serial killer. Some even claim that the murders were the result of a family feud or a botched robbery attempt.

Despite the numerous theories and the extensive investigation, the killer has never been identified. The case remains open, but due to its age, it is unlikely that it will ever be solved. The Hinterkaifeck murders have become a part of German folklore and continue to fascinate and intrigue true crime enthusiasts around the world.

The Hinterkaifeck murders are a haunting and unsettling case of murder that has baffled investigators for nearly a century. The brutality of the crime and the fact that the killer remained in the house for several days after the murders make this case truly unique and chilling. The case remains open, and while it is unlikely that the killer will ever be identified, the Hinterkaifeck murders will continue to captivate and terrify true crime enthusiasts for generations to come.

The Boy in the Box

The Boy in the Box is the name given to an unidentified young boy whose body was discovered in a cardboard box in a wooded area in Philadelphia, Pennsylvania in 1957. The case has remained unsolved for over six decades and has captured the attention of true crime enthusiasts and investigators alike.

On February 25, 1957, a young boy, estimated to be between 4 and 6 years old, was found dead in a cardboard box in the Fox Chase neighborhood of Philadelphia. The box had been left near Susquehanna Road and contained the body of the boy, who had been beaten and malnourished. The boy's hair had been cut recently and his nails had been trimmed, suggesting that someone had taken care of him before his death.

Despite an extensive investigation and widespread media attention, the boy's identity remains unknown to this day. He has been referred to by a number of different names over the years, including "America's Unknown Child," "The Boy in the Box," and "The Fox Chase Boy."

In the immediate aftermath of the discovery, the Philadelphia Police Department launched a massive investigation into the boy's death. They collected evidence from the box and the surrounding area and conducted interviews with potential witnesses. They also released a composite sketch of the boy in the hopes of identifying him.

Despite these efforts, no one came forward with information about the boy's identity or his killer. The investigation eventually went cold, but the case continued to generate public interest and media attention over the years.

In the decades since the boy's death, there have been numerous theories and potential leads in the case, but none have led to a definitive resolution. Some have suggested that the boy was the victim of child trafficking or abuse, while others believe he may have been the illegitimate child of a wealthy family. Some have even speculated that he may have been a victim of a cult or a serial killer.

One of the most intriguing potential leads in the case came in 2002, when a woman named Marge Everett came forward with a strange story. According to Everett, her abusive mother had purchased the boy from his birth parents and raised him as her own before killing him and disposing of his body in the cardboard box. While Everett's story was compelling, investigators were unable to find any concrete evidence to support her claims.

Despite the lack of resolution in the case, the boy's memory has been kept alive by a number of individuals and organizations over the years. In 1998, a group of volunteers in Philadelphia raised money to purchase a headstone for the boy's grave, which had previously been unmarked. The headstone reads "Heavenly Father, bless this unknown boy," and serves as a reminder of the ongoing search for justice in the case.

The Boy in the Box remains one of the most haunting unsolved mysteries in American true crime history. Despite the passage of time and the numerous potential leads and theories, the identity of the young boy and the circumstances surrounding his death continue to elude investigators. The case serves as a sobering reminder of the fragility of human life and the importance of seeking justice for those who cannot speak for themselves.

The Zodiac Killer

The Zodiac Killer is one of the most notorious and enigmatic serial killers in American history. Active in the late 1960s and early 1970s in Northern California, the Zodiac Killer was responsible for at least five murders, although he claimed to have killed as many as 37 people. The Zodiac Killer sent taunting letters to newspapers and police, which included cryptograms that he challenged people to solve. Despite extensive investigation, the identity of the Zodiac Killer has never been definitively confirmed.

The first confirmed attack by the Zodiac Killer was on December 20, 1968, when he shot and killed two high school students, Betty Lou Jensen and David Faraday, as they sat in a parked car in Benicia, California. Over the next year, the Zodiac Killer would strike three more times, killing two more people and seriously injuring two others. In each case, the killer used a gun, and in some cases, a knife.

What made the Zodiac Killer particularly disturbing was the way he taunted the police and the public. He sent a series of letters to newspapers, which included coded messages that he claimed would reveal his identity. In one letter, he wrote, "This is the Zodiac speaking. I like killing people because it is so much fun." The letters included details about the murders that only the killer would know, leading investigators to believe that they were authentic.

One of the most famous aspects of the Zodiac Killer case was the cryptograms he sent in his letters. The killer claimed that the cryptograms would reveal his identity, but despite extensive efforts by law enforcement and amateur codebreakers, only one of the cryptograms was definitively solved. The others remain unsolved to this day.

The case also had its share of false leads and suspects. One suspect, Arthur Leigh Allen, was investigated extensively but was ultimately cleared of any involvement in the murders. Other suspects have been suggested over the years, but none have been definitively proven to be the Zodiac Killer.

The last confirmed killing attributed to the Zodiac Killer occurred on October 11, 1969, when he shot and killed a cab driver named Paul Stine in San Francisco. After that, the killer continued to send letters but did not carry out any further attacks. The last known letter from the Zodiac Killer was sent in 1974.

Despite the extensive investigation and media attention the case received, the identity of the Zodiac Killer remains a mystery. Over the years, many theories and suspects have been put forward, but none have been proven. In recent years, advances in DNA technology have led to renewed efforts to solve the case. In 2018, a team of investigators claimed to have solved one of the Zodiac Killer's cryptograms, although their solution has not been widely accepted.

The Zodiac Killer case remains one of the most notorious unsolved mysteries in American history. The killer's taunting letters, cryptograms, and brazen attacks captured the public's imagination and have continued to fascinate people for decades. The case has been the subject of numerous books, movies, and documentaries, and has inspired countless amateur sleuths to try to crack the code and unmask the killer. Despite the passage of time, the case continues to captivate and intrigue, and the identity of the Zodiac Killer remains one of the greatest mysteries of our time.

The Chicago Tylenol Murders

The Chicago Tylenol Murders is a crime that shocked the United States in the 1980s. It was a series of murders that took place in the Chicago area, in which seven people died after taking Tylenol capsules laced with cyanide. The incident remains unsolved to this day, making it one of the most infamous unsolved crimes in American history.

The first victim of the Chicago Tylenol Murders was Mary Kellerman, a 12-year-old girl who died on September 29, 1982, after taking an Extra-Strength Tylenol capsule. That same day, Adam Janus, a 27-year-old postal worker, also died after taking a Tylenol capsule. His brother and sister-in-law, Stanley and Theresa Janus, died after taking Tylenol capsules from the same bottle.

As news of the deaths spread, panic set in. People across the country were afraid to take any medication that might be tampered with. The manufacturer of Tylenol, Johnson & Johnson, immediately issued a nationwide recall of all Tylenol capsules. The company also offered to exchange any Tylenol capsules that consumers had purchased for the safer Tylenol tablets.

The investigation into the Chicago Tylenol Murders was one of the most extensive in American history. The FBI, the FDA, and local law enforcement all worked together to try to solve the case. Despite their efforts, however, the killer was never found.

One of the theories put forth by investigators was that the killer had tampered with the Tylenol capsules in a store before they were sold. Another theory was that the killer had replaced the capsules in the bottles after they had been purchased. There was also speculation that the killer had a personal vendetta against Johnson & Johnson and was targeting the company.

In the aftermath of the murders, new packaging and safety measures were introduced for over-the-counter medications. The tamper-resistant packaging and safety seals we see on products today were largely a result of the Chicago Tylenol Murders.

Over the years, there have been several suspects in the case, but no one has ever been charged. In 2011, the FBI announced that it was reopening the case, but to this day, it remains unsolved.

The Chicago Tylenol Murders had a profound impact on American society. It was the first time that tampering with over-the-counter medications had resulted in multiple deaths. It created a sense of fear and mistrust that has lingered for decades. In many ways, it was a crime that changed the way we think about product safety and packaging.

The legacy of the Chicago Tylenol Murders lives on, even today. It serves as a reminder that even the most mundane products can be used for nefarious purposes. It also highlights the importance of thorough investigations and the need for justice for the victims and their families. The case remains one of the most significant unsolved crimes in American history and is likely to continue to captivate people's imaginations for years to come.

The Oklahoma Girl Scout Murders

The Oklahoma Girl Scout Murders is a chilling and disturbing case that has remained unsolved for over four decades. On June 13, 1977, three young girls were brutally murdered at Camp Scott, a Girl Scout camp located in Mayes County, Oklahoma. The victims, 8-year-old Lori Farmer, 9-year-old Michele Guse, and 10-year-old Denise Milner, were attending a two-week summer camp when they were killed in their tent during the night.

The tragedy shook the community and the nation, and the investigation into the murders became one of the largest in Oklahoma history. The crime scene was meticulously analyzed, and the police followed up on every lead and tip that came their way. Despite the massive efforts, the killer was never identified, and the case remains open to this day.

The investigation revealed that the killer had entered the girls' tent during the night and had used a flashlight to illuminate the scene. The girls had been bound and gagged, and their throats were slashed. The killer had then dragged the bodies out of the tent and left them in a wooded area near the camp. The brutal nature of the crime shocked the nation, and many were left wondering how such a heinous act could have taken place at a peaceful and idyllic summer camp.

In the days following the murders, the police received numerous tips and leads from the public, but none of them led to the identification of a suspect. The investigation hit a dead end until a local man, Gene Leroy Hart, was arrested for an unrelated charge. Hart was a convicted rapist and had been on the run from authorities for several years. He had a history of violence and was known to be in the area at the time of the murders.

The police quickly focused their attention on Hart and conducted a thorough investigation into his possible involvement in the Girl Scout murders. They found several pieces of evidence that linked Hart to the crime, including a hair that was found on one of the victims' clothing that was a match for his. However, the prosecution's case was largely circumstantial, and Hart's defense team argued that the evidence was not enough to convict him.

In 1979, Hart was tried for the murders of the three girls, but the jury was unable to reach a verdict. He was acquitted of the charges, and the case remained unsolved. Hart died a year later from a heart attack, and the investigation into the Oklahoma Girl Scout Murders was officially closed.

Over the years, the case has been revisited by investigators and amateur sleuths, but no new leads or evidence have emerged. Theories about the identity of the killer abound, and some have speculated that Hart was not the only one involved in the crime. Others have suggested that the murders were part of a larger conspiracy or that the killer was a member of the local community.

Despite the lack of resolution, the Oklahoma Girl Scout Murders remain one of the most tragic and disturbing cases in American true crime history. The brutal and senseless killing of three young girls has left an indelible mark on the community and serves as a reminder of the importance of justice and the need to hold those who commit such heinous crimes accountable.

The JonBenét Ramsey Murder

The murder of JonBenét Ramsey is a case that has captivated the world for over two decades. On December 26, 1996, the six-year-old beauty queen was found dead in her family's home in Boulder, Colorado. The case remains unsolved to this day, and many theories have been proposed about who killed JonBenét and why.

JonBenét was born in Atlanta, Georgia in 1990. Her parents, John and Patsy Ramsey, were a wealthy couple who had made their fortune in the computer industry. The family moved to Boulder, Colorado in 1991, and JonBenét quickly became involved in the local beauty pageant circuit. In 1995, she won the title of Little Miss Colorado.

The events leading up to JonBenét's murder are shrouded in mystery. On the night of December 25, 1996, the Ramsey family attended a Christmas party at a friend's house. They returned home around midnight, and put JonBenét to bed. The next morning, Patsy Ramsey called the police to report that her daughter had been kidnapped, and that a ransom note had been left behind.

When police arrived at the Ramsey home, they found the ransom note on a staircase leading to the basement. The note demanded $118,000 in exchange for JonBenét's safe return, and warned that the family should not contact the police or JonBenét would be killed. However, despite the ransom note, JonBenét's body was found later that day in the basement of the Ramsey home.

The cause of JonBenét's death was determined to be strangulation, and her body showed signs of sexual assault. The investigation quickly turned to the Ramsey family, as there were several inconsistencies in their story. For example, the ransom note was written on a notepad found in the Ramsey home, and experts determined that it had been written by Patsy Ramsey. In addition, the

Ramsey's son, Burke, was in the house at the time of the murder, and his fingerprints were found on a bowl of pineapple that was found in the kitchen.

Despite these inconsistencies, the case remains unsolved to this day. The Boulder Police Department has been criticized for mishandling the investigation, and for focusing too heavily on the Ramsey family as suspects. Many theories have been proposed about who killed JonBenét, including intruders, family friends, and even members of the Ramsey family themselves.

In 2016, CBS aired a docu-series called "The Case of: JonBenét Ramsey," which reexamined the evidence and presented a theory that JonBenét's older brother, Burke, had accidentally killed her, and that the Ramsey family had covered it up. However, this theory has been disputed by many, and the case remains open.

The JonBenét Ramsey murder has been the subject of numerous books, movies, and TV shows. The case has captivated the public's attention for over two decades, and many people continue to believe that the truth about what happened that fateful night has yet to be uncovered.

The murder of JonBenét Ramsey is one of the most notorious unsolved crimes in American history. The circumstances surrounding her death are shrouded in mystery, and the investigation has been plagued by controversy and mishandling. Despite numerous theories and investigations, the case remains unsolved to this day. The murder of JonBenét Ramsey is a tragic reminder of the dangers that can lurk in even the most seemingly safe and affluent communities, and a testament to the enduring power of true crime to captivate the public's attention.

The Villisca Axe Murders

The Villisca Axe Murders is a true crime story that still haunts the small town of Villisca, Iowa over a century later. It is a tale of unspeakable violence that occurred in the early morning hours of June 10, 1912, when eight people were bludgeoned to death with an axe inside their own home.

The victims were the Moore family, consisting of parents Josiah and Sarah, their four children, and two young girls who were friends of the family. All eight were asleep when the attacker entered the home and committed the heinous act. The killer used both the sharp and blunt ends of the axe to inflict devastating blows on the heads of each victim, making sure to cover the mirrors and windows before leaving the house.

The investigation that followed was plagued by mishandling of evidence and a lack of forensic knowledge. The crime scene was trampled by curious onlookers before the police arrived, and the coroner arrived hours later. It was later discovered that two people had been sleeping in the guest room of the home at the time of the murders but were not discovered until the morning. Furthermore, multiple suspects were identified over the years, but no one was ever charged with the crime.

The town of Villisca was left in shock and fear following the murders. Rumors and gossip spread like wildfire, and the town was swarmed by journalists, investigators, and curiosity seekers. In an effort to find the killer, locals formed vigilante groups, and some were even accused of committing the murders themselves.

The crime scene is now a popular tourist attraction and has been restored to its original state, complete with the furniture and personal belongings of the Moore family. The axe used in the murders, however, has never been found.

Over the years, numerous theories have been put forth about who committed the Villisca Axe Murders. One theory involves a traveling minister who was in town the night of the murders and was known to carry an axe. Another theory is that the killer was a serial killer who had committed similar crimes in other towns. There are also theories that the murders were committed by a disgruntled employee of Josiah Moore's or even by a member of the Ku Klux Klan.

Despite the countless theories and investigations, the Villisca Axe Murders remain unsolved to this day. The brutal killings have left a lasting impact on the town of Villisca and have become part of American true crime lore. The case has been the subject of numerous books, TV shows, and movies, and has been studied by criminologists and forensic experts alike.

The Villisca Axe Murders stand as a haunting reminder of the brutality and darkness that can exist within the human psyche. It is a crime that has yet to be solved, and one that continues to fascinate and terrify people to this day.

The O.J. Simpson Murder Trial

The O.J. Simpson murder trial is one of the most famous and controversial criminal trials in American history. It was a case that captured the attention of the entire nation and divided it along racial lines. At the center of it all was a former professional football player and actor, O.J. Simpson, who was accused of murdering his ex-wife, Nicole Brown Simpson, and her friend, Ron Goldman, in the early morning hours of June 12, 1994.

The crime was a brutal one. Brown Simpson and Goldman were found stabbed to death outside of Brown Simpson's home in Brentwood, a wealthy Los Angeles suburb. Simpson was immediately a person of interest in the case, given his tumultuous relationship with Brown Simpson and the fact that he had a history of domestic violence. He was soon charged with the murders, and what followed was a trial that would last nearly a year and become a media circus.

The trial began on January 24, 1995, and quickly became a spectacle. It was the first trial in history to be broadcast on live television, with millions of Americans tuning in to watch the proceedings. The prosecution argued that Simpson had motive, opportunity, and means to commit the murders. They presented DNA evidence, blood stains, and a glove found at the scene that they claimed linked Simpson to the crime.

The defense, led by a team of high-profile attorneys including Robert Shapiro and Johnnie Cochran, argued that Simpson was being framed by a racist police department and that the evidence against him was circumstantial. They also famously employed the tactic of casting doubt on the reliability of the DNA evidence, questioning whether it had been contaminated or mishandled.

Throughout the trial, tensions ran high. The case was not just about Simpson's guilt or innocence, but also about issues of race and policing in America. Many African Americans saw the case as an example of systemic racism in the criminal justice system, and they rallied behind Simpson as a symbol of resistance. Meanwhile, many white Americans saw Simpson as a cold-blooded killer who was trying to use his celebrity status to get away with murder.

The trial lasted for nearly a year and was full of dramatic moments. Perhaps the most infamous was the moment when Simpson tried on the leather gloves found at the crime scene in front of the jury. The gloves were too small and did not fit, leading Cochran to famously quip, "If it doesn't fit, you must acquit."

In the end, the jury found Simpson not guilty of the murders. The verdict was met with both jubilation and outrage, with many African Americans celebrating Simpson's acquittal as a victory against a racist justice system, while many white Americans saw it as a miscarriage of justice. The trial had revealed deep-seated racial tensions in America, and it had also changed the way that criminal trials were covered by the media.

In the years since the trial, there has been ongoing debate about Simpson's guilt or innocence. Many people still believe that he got away with murder, while others believe that he was the victim of a racist police department and a flawed justice system. Regardless of one's opinion, the O.J. Simpson trial remains a watershed moment in American history, one that exposed the deep-seated racial tensions in the country and forever changed the way that we view high-profile criminal trials.

Bizarre Burglaries

The Naptime Burglar

The world of crime is full of bizarre and unusual cases, and the Naptime Burglar is no exception. This criminal is known for breaking into homes, but instead of stealing valuables, they take the opportunity to catch up on some much-needed rest.

The first reported case of the Naptime Burglar occurred in 2009 in St. Louis, Missouri. A family returned home to find their house in disarray and assumed that they had been robbed. However, upon closer inspection, they realized that nothing had been stolen, and the only evidence of the break-in was a stranger fast asleep on their couch.

Police were called to the scene, and the burglar was apprehended without incident. The intruder was identified as a 35-year-old man who had been homeless and looking for a place to rest. He had broken into the home through a window and had made himself at home on the family's couch.

This case was unique not only because the burglar didn't steal anything, but also because he made himself at home in such a casual way. The homeowner reported that the intruder had even made himself a sandwich before nodding off.

But the Naptime Burglar didn't stop there. In 2012, a man in Massachusetts returned home to find his house in a similar state of disarray. He discovered a stranger sleeping in his bed and quickly called the police.

When the police arrived, they found the burglar fast asleep, surrounded by several items that he had taken from the house, including a watch, a pair of sunglasses, and a small amount of cash. The burglar was arrested, and it was later discovered that he had a history of breaking into homes in the area to take naps.

In another case, a woman in Seattle, Washington, returned home to find a man sleeping in her bed. The burglar had entered the home through an unlocked window and had made himself at home, even going so far as to take a shower before settling in for a nap.

The homeowner, understandably shaken, called the police, and the man was taken into custody. It was later discovered that the burglar had a history of breaking into homes to sleep and had been arrested for similar crimes in the past.

While the Naptime Burglar's crimes may seem harmless compared to other burglars who steal valuables or cause damage, the fact remains that they are still breaking into homes illegally. In some cases, homeowners may feel violated or uneasy knowing that a stranger has entered their home, even if nothing was stolen.

The Naptime Burglar's crimes also highlight a larger issue of homelessness and the need for safe and accessible places for individuals to rest. It's important to note that the Naptime Burglar was homeless and likely entered homes to find a safe place to sleep. This raises questions about the lack of resources and support for individuals experiencing homelessness and the need for communities to address these issues.

The Naptime Burglar is a prime example of a bizarre burglary that, while not necessarily harmful, still highlights important social and criminal justice issues. The need for safe and accessible resources for individuals experiencing homelessness is clear, and addressing these issues can help prevent similar crimes from occurring in the future.

The Toilet Seat Thief

The act of burglary is already considered bizarre and illegal, but some individuals take it to another level by stealing peculiar items. A classic example is the toilet seat thief, who only targets this bathroom fixture.

The first recorded incident of the toilet seat theft happened in 1995 in a small town in Illinois. The homeowners noticed that their toilet seat was missing and reported it to the authorities. The police were puzzled, as there were no signs of forced entry and nothing else was taken from the house. It seemed that the burglar only had one intention - to steal the toilet seat.

The news of the toilet seat theft quickly spread, and it caught the attention of the media. The public found it amusing and bizarre, and it even became a trending topic in talk shows and news programs. However, as time passed, the case became more serious as it continued to happen in different parts of the country.

In the early 2000s, the toilet seat thief struck again, this time in a university campus in Michigan. The thief stole over 150 toilet seats, causing an estimated $10,000 in damages. It was a huge inconvenience for the students and faculty, as they had to replace the toilet seats one by one.

The authorities were determined to catch the toilet seat thief, but the case remained unsolved for years. It wasn't until 2005 when they finally got a break. The police received a tip from a neighbor who saw a man carrying a toilet seat in the middle of the night. The police quickly apprehended the suspect, and he was found to have dozens of toilet seats in his possession.

The man, who was identified as a local plumber, admitted to stealing over 200 toilet seats in the span of ten years. He claimed that he was obsessed with collecting toilet seats, and he found pleasure in stealing them from different locations. He even had a storage room filled with toilet seats, which he displayed like trophies.

The toilet seat thief's case may seem bizarre, but it is not an isolated incident. There have been reports of similar cases around the world, with burglars targeting toilet seats, toilet paper, and other bathroom items. In 2013, a man in Germany was arrested for stealing over 200 rolls of toilet paper from public restrooms. He claimed that he did it because he couldn't afford to buy toilet paper himself.

These bizarre burglaries may seem harmless, but they can cause significant inconvenience and cost to the victims. For instance, the theft of toilet seats can cause damage to the toilet itself, which requires costly repairs. The theft of toilet paper, on the other hand, can disrupt public services and cause a shortage in supply.

The toilet seat thief's case is a prime example of how bizarre burglaries can become an obsession for some individuals. It is not just about the monetary value of the items being stolen, but rather the thrill of getting away with something unusual and bizarre. It is a form of deviant behavior that stems from psychological issues, such as compulsive hoarding or kleptomania.

The toilet seat thief is just one of the many bizarre burglaries that have been reported throughout history. It may seem amusing and harmless, but it is a serious crime that causes inconvenience and harm to the victims. The case also highlights the psychological issues behind this kind of behavior, which should be addressed through proper intervention and treatment.

The Honey Heist

In 2018, New Zealand experienced an unusual crime spree involving a precious commodity - honey. The country is known for its delicious and high-quality Manuka honey, which is in high demand both domestically and internationally. However, it was not the Manuka honey that was the target of the honey heist. Instead, it was a different type of honey - Kanuka honey, produced by the Kiwi Beez company.

The heist occurred on February 22, 2018, at Kiwi Beez's warehouse in the town of Te Awamutu. The burglars cut a hole in the fence surrounding the property and broke into the warehouse. They then stole 24 barrels of Kanuka honey, weighing a total of 600 kilograms (1,320 pounds). The value of the stolen honey was estimated to be around $60,000 NZD (approximately $41,000 USD).

The heist was particularly brazen, as the burglars had to move the barrels out of the warehouse and load them onto a vehicle. The theft was discovered the following morning, and the police were immediately informed. A spokesperson for Kiwi Beez described the theft as "gut-wrenching" for the small, family-owned business.

The police investigation into the honey heist led them to a group of suspects who were known to be involved in the illegal trade of Manuka honey. Manuka honey has a higher value than Kanuka honey and is often targeted by thieves. However, in this case, it was discovered that the Kanuka honey had been stolen to order for a group of local buyers who were looking to purchase the honey at a discounted price.

The police eventually arrested and charged three people in connection with the heist. Two men and a woman were charged with burglary and receiving stolen property. They were sentenced to a combined total of 11 years in prison.

The Kanuka honey heist was not the first of its kind in New Zealand. In 2017, a group of thieves stole more than $100,000 NZD (approximately $69,000 USD) worth of Manuka honey from a warehouse in the town of Hamilton. The theft occurred over several nights, and the burglars cut through fences and walls to gain access to the honey. They also disabled the alarm system and CCTV cameras.

The demand for honey in New Zealand has led to an increase in honey-related crimes. In addition to burglaries, there have been instances of honey tampering, where individuals have adulterated honey with cheaper ingredients to sell it at a higher price. There have also been cases of honey laundering, where honey is imported from other countries and then relabeled as New Zealand honey to take advantage of its higher value.

The honey heist in New Zealand is just one example of how unusual crimes can occur even in seemingly ordinary industries. The high value of honey, particularly Manuka honey, has led to a rise in honey-related crimes, and the police have had to adapt their methods to combat this trend.

The honey heist in New Zealand is a fascinating example of a bizarre burglary. The theft of 24 barrels of Kanuka honey may seem relatively minor in the grand scheme of things, but it had a significant impact on the small business that was targeted. The fact that the heist was carried out to order by a group of local buyers shows how unusual crimes can occur in unexpected ways. As long as there are valuable commodities, there will be those who seek to profit from them through illegal means.

The Cereal Killer

The world of crime is filled with strange and bizarre incidents that often leave people scratching their heads in confusion. In 2014, one such incident occurred in Massachusetts, USA, that had people both amused and perplexed at the same time. It involved a man who had broken into a home and stolen boxes of cereal, earning him the nickname "The Cereal Killer."

The story of the Cereal Killer began on a typical day in May when the homeowners returned to their residence in Marlborough, Massachusetts, only to find that their home had been burglarized. While the homeowners were certainly upset about the intrusion, what made the burglary so strange was that the thief had only stolen boxes of cereal.

The police were called, and they quickly began investigating the crime scene. After gathering evidence, the investigators soon discovered that the burglar had broken into the home through a window and had taken nothing but boxes of cereal from the kitchen pantry. This bizarre and seemingly pointless theft left the authorities baffled.

However, the mystery of the Cereal Killer was soon solved when the police received a tip from a local resident. The tipster informed the authorities that a man had been seen walking around the neighborhood carrying several boxes of cereal.

The police followed up on this lead and were able to identify the man as Robert Owens, a 22-year-old from Framingham, Massachusetts. Owens had a history of drug abuse and had been arrested several times before for various offenses. After he was arrested, Owens admitted to the burglary and explained that he had been looking for food to steal.

Despite Owens' confession, many people were still left puzzled by his actions. Why would someone break into a home and steal boxes of cereal? It seemed like an incredibly strange thing to do.

Some people speculated that Owens might have been suffering from a mental illness or that he was simply desperate for food. Others wondered if he was playing a prank or if there was some deeper meaning behind the theft.

Whatever the reason behind the Cereal Killer's actions, one thing was certain: the incident had captured the public's attention. People all over the country were talking about the strange burglary and wondering what could have motivated someone to break into a home just to steal cereal.

The incident also raised questions about the nature of crime and criminal behavior. It's not uncommon for thieves to target expensive or valuable items, such as jewelry, electronics, or cash. But stealing cereal? That seemed like an entirely different level of strange.

Perhaps the Cereal Killer's actions were simply the result of desperation or a momentary lapse in judgment. Or maybe there was a more complex psychological explanation behind the burglary. Either way, the incident served as a reminder that the world of crime is full of unexpected surprises and bizarre incidents.

In the end, Robert Owens was sentenced to two and a half years in prison for his crime. But even after his conviction, people continued to talk about the strange case of the Cereal Killer. It had become a symbol of the strange and unpredictable nature of crime, and it would undoubtedly be remembered for years to come.

The Cheeseburglar

In 2009, a string of burglaries occurred in the city of Fremont, California that left residents puzzled and law enforcement scratching their heads. The thief, dubbed the "Cheeseburglar" by the local media, had a unique modus operandi: breaking into homes solely to steal frozen cheeseburgers.

The Cheeseburglar's crime spree began in early January of that year, when a homeowner in the Ardenwood neighborhood of Fremont reported that someone had broken into their garage and stolen several boxes of frozen White Castle cheeseburgers. The incident seemed like a random act of petty theft, but it was only the beginning.

Over the next several weeks, more burglaries were reported in the same neighborhood. In each case, the only items taken were boxes of frozen cheeseburgers from the victims' freezers. The burglar seemed to have a preference for White Castle burgers, but also took other brands if they were available.

The Cheeseburglar's actions left the residents of Fremont bewildered. Why would someone go to such lengths to steal frozen hamburgers? Was it some kind of bizarre prank or dare? Or was there something more sinister at play?

Law enforcement took the matter seriously and began investigating the burglaries. They interviewed neighbors, collected evidence from the crime scenes, and even set up surveillance cameras in an attempt to catch the perpetrator. But despite their efforts, the Cheeseburglar remained elusive.

It wasn't until late February that police finally got a break in the case. A man was caught attempting to break into a home in the same neighborhood where the previous burglaries had occurred. When police searched the man's car, they found several boxes of frozen cheeseburgers from various brands, including White Castle.

The man, identified as 32-year-old Kareem Watt of Fremont, was arrested and charged with multiple counts of burglary. During his interrogation, Watt admitted to the cheeseburger thefts, claiming that he had a "craving" for them and couldn't afford to buy them himself.

Watt's confession may have explained his motive, but it still left many questions unanswered. Why did he target the same neighborhood repeatedly? And why only steal frozen cheeseburgers?

The Cheeseburglar's crimes may seem amusing or even harmless, but they had a real impact on the victims. The stolen food represented more than just a minor inconvenience; for some, it was a significant loss of money and a violation of their homes.

Kareem Watt was sentenced to three years in prison for his string of cheeseburger burglaries. While the case may have seemed like a trivial matter at first glance, it served as a reminder that even the most seemingly innocuous crimes can have serious consequences.

The Cheeseburglar's strange actions also highlighted the unusual nature of some burglaries. While most burglars target homes for valuable items like cash and jewelry, there are those who steal for more unusual reasons. Whether it's a naptime burglar or a toilet seat thief, these crimes may seem comical or even absurd, but they still have victims and consequences.

The Cheeseburglar may have gotten his fix of frozen cheeseburgers, but he also got a criminal record and a prison sentence. His actions serve as a cautionary tale about the unexpected and bizarre nature of some crimes, and the importance of taking even seemingly minor thefts seriously.

The Snowman Burglar

The Snowman Burglar was a notorious thief who gained notoriety in Sweden for his unusual methods of breaking into homes during the winter season. He would leave behind a calling card in the form of a snowman near the scene of the crime, hence earning the nickname 'The Snowman Burglar'.

Between 2005 and 2006, the Snowman Burglar committed a series of burglaries in the small town of Torsby in Värmland, Sweden. During this time, he broke into over 20 homes, stealing cash, jewellery, and other valuable items.

What made the Snowman Burglar so unique was his method of breaking in. Instead of forcing his way in, he would often enter the home through a window or door that was left unlocked. Once inside, he would steal items that were easy to carry, such as cash, jewellery, and electronics.

Despite the fact that the Snowman Burglar left behind a distinctive calling card, he managed to evade capture for several months. In fact, it wasn't until he made a mistake that he was finally caught.

In January 2006, the Snowman Burglar broke into a home in Torsby and stole a large amount of cash. However, as he was leaving the scene of the crime, he slipped on the ice and dropped some of the money. The police were able to use the dropped money to track him down and arrest him.

After his arrest, the Snowman Burglar confessed to committing over 20 burglaries in Torsby. He explained that he had been stealing items to fund his drug addiction, and that he chose to leave the snowman as a calling card because he thought it was funny.

The Snowman Burglar was eventually sentenced to two years in prison for his crimes. However, his story did not end there.

In 2012, the Snowman Burglar was released from prison and moved to a small village in Norway. There, he started a new life and tried to put his criminal past behind him. However, his reputation as the Snowman Burglar had preceded him, and he was soon recognized by some of the locals.

Despite his attempts to start anew, the Snowman Burglar was unable to escape his past. In 2013, he was found dead in his apartment, the victim of an apparent drug overdose. His death marked the end of a strange and unusual criminal career that had baffled police and captivated the public for years.

The Snowman Burglar may have been a small-time thief, but his unique methods and calling card made him stand out from the rest. His story serves as a reminder that even the most seemingly innocuous crimes can have a lasting impact on those involved, and that the consequences of our actions can follow us for years to come.

The Naked Burglar

In 2004, a man known as the "Naked Burglar" made headlines across the United States for a string of bizarre break-ins. The perpetrator, 49-year-old Mark Rubinson, had a unique modus operandi: he would break into homes and businesses completely naked.

Rubinson's first known offense occurred in November 2003 when he broke into a tanning salon in Lakewood, Colorado. He managed to steal $70 in cash and a few tanning products before fleeing the scene. The salon owner found the break-in strange, but assumed it was just a random act of vandalism.

However, Rubinson continued his naked burglary spree over the next several months. He hit a variety of targets, including a dance studio, a coffee shop, and a flower shop. His most audacious burglary occurred in March 2004 when he broke into a dental office in the middle of the night.

Once inside, Rubinson removed all of his clothes and proceeded to steal a number of items, including a camera, a computer, and several checks. He then defecated on the floor of the office before leaving the scene.

Despite his strange and messy behavior, Rubinson managed to evade arrest for several months. However, his luck ran out in June 2004 when he was caught in the act of breaking into a business in Denver.

Police were able to track Rubinson down thanks to a witness who reported seeing a naked man in the area. When officers arrived, they found Rubinson breaking into a building and took him into custody.

During his interrogation, Rubinson admitted to committing more than 20 burglaries in the Denver area over the previous several months. He explained that he would strip down before breaking into buildings in order to avoid leaving any incriminating evidence, such as fibers from his clothing.

Rubinson's bizarre burglary spree earned him a great deal of media attention, with many news outlets dubbing him the "Naked Burglar." His story became a topic of national discussion, with many people speculating about what could have motivated him to commit such unusual crimes.

Some experts suggested that Rubinson may have been suffering from a mental illness or an addiction to exhibitionism. Others argued that he was simply seeking attention or experiencing a midlife crisis.

In any case, Rubinson's naked burglaries came to an end in December 2004 when he pleaded guilty to 11 counts of burglary and was sentenced to 11 years in prison. He was also required to register as a sex offender upon his release.

Today, the Naked Burglar remains a memorable figure in the history of strange crimes. His bizarre behavior and unusual methods of burglary have cemented his place as one of the most memorable criminals of recent years.

The Watermelon Thief

Theft can come in all shapes and sizes. From petty theft to grand larceny, the act of stealing can range from the mundane to the bizarre. In the case of the Watermelon Thief, it was the latter.

In the summer of 2019, a small town in Alabama was rocked by a series of thefts that seemed to come out of nowhere. The thefts were not of cars, electronics, or money, but of watermelons. Yes, watermelons.

The Watermelon Thief, as he came to be known, targeted small roadside stands that sold fresh produce. He would sneak in under the cover of darkness and make off with as many watermelons as he could carry. The thief was never caught, and the town was left wondering who could be behind such a strange and seemingly harmless crime.

As the summer wore on, the Watermelon Thief became bolder. He began to target larger farms and would take not just a few watermelons, but entire crops. Some farmers reported losses in the thousands of dollars. The Watermelon Thief was not just a quirky thief; he was becoming a serious problem for the community.

As news of the thefts spread, the town rallied together to catch the Watermelon Thief. Farmers and locals banded together to patrol the roads and keep an eye out for any suspicious activity. Some even set up cameras and motion sensors in their fields to try and catch the thief in the act.

The Watermelon Thief remained elusive, however. He seemed to know when and where to strike, and always managed to evade capture. The town was becoming frustrated and angry, with some calling for the police to get involved.

Eventually, the Watermelon Thief made a mistake. He was caught on camera at a local farm, and the footage was clear enough to identify him. It turned out that the Watermelon Thief was a local man who had fallen on hard times. He had lost his job and was struggling to make ends meet, and he saw stealing watermelons as a way to provide for his family.

The Watermelon Thief was arrested and charged with theft. He pleaded guilty and was sentenced to community service and probation. The town was relieved that the thief had been caught, but also saddened that a member of their own community had been forced to resort to such desperate measures.

The Watermelon Thief may have been an odd and seemingly harmless criminal, but his actions had a real impact on the community. The farmers who lost crops suffered financial losses, and the sense of security in the town was shaken. It goes to show that even the most unusual crimes can have serious consequences.

In the end, the Watermelon Thief served his sentence and was able to get back on his feet. The town moved on, but the memory of the strange watermelon heist lingered. It was a reminder that crime can come in all shapes and sizes, and that even the most unexpected criminals can cause real harm.

The Golf Club Thief

In 2018, a man in Florida was arrested for stealing over 100 golf clubs from various golf courses in the area. The thief, identified as Mark Allen Smith, had been breaking into golf club storage rooms and stealing the clubs for months before he was caught.

The thefts had become a major problem for the local golf community, with thousands of dollars worth of equipment being stolen. Smith's modus operandi was to break into the storage rooms at night, and carefully select the most expensive clubs. He would then sell the clubs on the internet or at pawn shops for a fraction of their value.

The thefts had gone on for so long that many of the local golf courses had started to take extra security measures. Some had installed security cameras, while others had hired additional security guards to patrol the property at night. Despite this, Smith managed to evade detection for months.

It was not until one of the golf course managers noticed a suspicious Craigslist ad for a set of golf clubs that the police were able to track down Smith. The manager contacted the police, who set up a sting operation to catch Smith in the act. When Smith arrived to sell the stolen clubs, he was arrested and charged with multiple counts of grand theft.

During the investigation, police discovered that Smith had been using the money from the stolen clubs to fund his gambling addiction. He had racked up thousands of dollars in gambling debts and had turned to stealing as a way to pay them off.

The golf club thefts caused a lot of frustration and anger in the local golf community. Many golfers were left without their favorite clubs and had to spend a lot of money to replace them. Some even started to take their clubs home with them after each game to prevent them from being stolen.

The case also highlighted the growing problem of theft in the golfing world. Golf clubs are valuable items, and thefts are becoming increasingly common. Many golf courses are now taking extra measures to protect their equipment, including installing security cameras, hiring additional security guards, and requiring proof of ownership before allowing golfers to use rental clubs.

The case of the golf club thief serves as a reminder of the importance of security in all aspects of our lives, and the need to take action to prevent theft and protect our valuable possessions. It also shows how addiction can lead people down dangerous paths and cause them to do things they never would have imagined.

Smith was sentenced to several years in prison for his crimes. The stolen golf clubs were returned to their rightful owners, and the local golf community breathed a sigh of relief knowing that the thief was off the streets. However, the case serves as a cautionary tale to always be vigilant and protect our valuables, no matter how mundane they may seem.

The Chicken Wing Bandit

The Chicken Wing Bandit is an infamous criminal who made headlines in 2016 for his bizarre burglary of a popular restaurant chain in Georgia, USA. This unusual heist earned him the title of the "Chicken Wing Bandit" and left law enforcement puzzled by his unusual motive.

On March 21, 2016, the Chicken Wing Bandit broke into a branch of the American Deli chain in the city of Lithonia. The burglar, whose identity remains unknown to this day, was caught on surveillance footage crawling on his hands and knees through the restaurant's ductwork before dropping down into the kitchen. Once inside, the bandit went straight for the restaurant's prized possession: the chicken wings.

The thief made off with a total of $4,000 worth of chicken wings, which amounted to approximately 150 pounds of meat. In addition to the chicken wings, the Chicken Wing Bandit also stole $1,000 in cash from the restaurant.

The burglary was reported to the police the following day, and investigators immediately began their search for the culprit. The surveillance footage of the burglary quickly went viral, with news outlets across the country reporting on the bizarre crime. The Chicken Wing Bandit became an internet sensation, with many people expressing their amusement at the strange and unusual nature of the burglary.

As the police investigation continued, they received an unexpected break in the case when a man was arrested for selling stolen chicken wings to local businesses. The man, who was not identified as the Chicken Wing Bandit, told investigators that he had purchased the chicken wings from an unknown person and had no knowledge of the burglary. Despite this lead, the police were unable to make any arrests in connection with the case.

The Chicken Wing Bandit's motives for the burglary remain a mystery to this day. Some speculate that he may have been a disgruntled employee seeking revenge on the restaurant, while others believe that he was simply a chicken wing enthusiast with a serious craving. The bizarre nature of the crime has made it one of the most memorable and talked-about burglaries in recent history.

The Chicken Wing Bandit's story has become the stuff of legend, with many people finding humor in the unusual crime. Memes and jokes about the Chicken Wing Bandit continue to circulate online, with people making light of the situation and poking fun at the thief's love of chicken wings.

Despite the humor and amusement surrounding the Chicken Wing Bandit, it is important to remember that burglary is a serious crime that can have serious consequences. The theft of property, whether it be chicken wings or cash, can have a significant impact on businesses and individuals. The Chicken Wing Bandit's crime may have been unusual and amusing, but it still had a real and negative impact on the American Deli chain.

The Chicken Wing Bandit's burglary of the American Deli chain in Georgia was a bizarre and unusual crime that left many people scratching their heads in confusion. The thief's love of chicken wings and unusual method of breaking into the restaurant made him an internet sensation, with many people finding humor in the situation. While the Chicken Wing Bandit's story may be amusing, it is important to remember that burglary is a serious crime with serious consequences.

Oddball Arsons

The Pillow Pyro

The Pillow Pyro was a serial arsonist who terrorized the city of Los Angeles in the mid-1980s. The arsonist's preferred method was to set fire to pillows that were left outside of people's homes. While this might seem like a strange choice of object to ignite, the Pillow Pyro was responsible for over 40 fires, causing hundreds of thousands of dollars in damage.

The Pillow Pyro was first noticed by the Los Angeles Fire Department in 1984. At that time, firefighters began responding to a string of small fires in the Hollywood and West Hollywood areas. While these fires didn't cause much damage, they were all started by someone lighting a pillow on fire and leaving it outside of a home or business.

As the number of fires increased, the authorities began to take the Pillow Pyro's actions more seriously. The Los Angeles Police Department and the Los Angeles Fire Department launched a joint investigation, and a task force was created to catch the arsonist.

Despite the task force's best efforts, the Pillow Pyro remained at large for months. He continued to strike in different neighborhoods throughout Los Angeles, and the authorities were unable to identify any suspects.

The situation came to a head in 1985 when the Pillow Pyro escalated his attacks. On August 31 of that year, he set fire to a three-story apartment building in Hollywood, causing over $1 million in damage. Fortunately, no one was injured in the fire, but it was clear that the arsonist was becoming more dangerous.

In the wake of the apartment building fire, the authorities redoubled their efforts to catch the Pillow Pyro. They began interviewing witnesses and analyzing evidence from the crime scenes. Finally, in September 1985, they got a break in the case.

A woman named Dorothea Puente was arrested on suspicion of running a boarding house where she had murdered her tenants and buried their bodies in the yard. During her arrest, police found a pillowcase in her possession that matched the ones used by the Pillow Pyro in his fires.

Further investigation revealed that Puente had a history of setting fires and had been living in the Hollywood area at the time of the Pillow Pyro's attacks. While there was never any direct evidence linking her to the fires, the circumstantial evidence was strong enough to convince the authorities that she was the culprit.

In 1986, Puente was convicted of three counts of arson and sentenced to five years in prison. While she was never officially charged with the Pillow Pyro fires, the authorities believe that she was responsible for them.

The Pillow Pyro's reign of terror came to an end thanks to the tireless efforts of the Los Angeles Fire Department, the Los Angeles Police Department, and the task force that was created to catch him. While the damage caused by the fires was significant, the fact that no one was injured is a testament to the skill of the firefighters who responded to the scenes.

The Pillow Pyro's choice of weapon was unusual, but it was also incredibly dangerous. Fires caused by pillows can spread quickly, and they are difficult to extinguish. The fact that the Pillow Pyro was able to remain at large for as long as he did is a testament to his cunning and ability to evade capture.

Today, the Pillow Pyro is just a memory, but his legacy lives on. He serves as a reminder of the damage that can be caused by arsonists, and the importance of catching them before they can cause more harm. The Pillow Pyro may have been an oddball, but he was also a criminal who put lives and property at risk.

The Toilet Paper Torch

In 2020, the world faced a shortage of toilet paper due to panic-buying caused by the COVID-19 pandemic. People across the globe were hoarding toilet paper, causing shortages in stores and supermarkets. During this time, a bizarre incident occurred in a small town in Massachusetts, USA that shocked the community and made national headlines.

The incident involved a man named John, who had a history of mental illness. John had been living alone in a small house on the outskirts of town for several years. He was known to his neighbors as a recluse who rarely left his home or interacted with anyone.

One evening, neighbors noticed a strange smell coming from John's house. Soon after, smoke was seen billowing from the windows. The fire department was called, and they arrived at the scene to find John's house engulfed in flames.

After the firefighters had put out the fire, they discovered that the blaze had been started by a bizarre method. John had used toilet paper to set his house on fire. He had soaked rolls of toilet paper in gasoline and strategically placed them around his home before setting them ablaze.

John was taken into custody and charged with arson. During his interrogation, he told the police that he had started the fire because he was angry at the world and wanted to watch everything burn. He also claimed that he had used toilet paper because it was readily available, and he thought it would be a quick and effective way to start a fire.

This strange case of arson raised several questions. How did John manage to acquire gasoline? Did he plan the fire in advance? Was his mental illness a factor in his actions? The investigation revealed that John had purchased gasoline from a nearby gas station the day before the fire. It also revealed that he had been planning the fire for several days and had strategically placed the toilet paper rolls around his home to ensure maximum damage.

The incident left the town in shock and disbelief. The community was unable to understand why someone would commit such a heinous crime. The shortage of toilet paper caused by the pandemic had caused many inconveniences, but no one had expected it to lead to such a bizarre incident.

The Toilet Paper Torch is just one example of the oddball arsons that have occurred throughout history. Arson is a serious crime that can cause significant damage to property and even lead to loss of life. However, when the motivation for arson is unusual or bizarre, it can leave people scratching their heads and wondering what could have possibly motivated the perpetrator.

The motives for arson can be complex and varied. In some cases, it may be motivated by revenge, anger, or financial gain. In other cases, it may be due to mental illness, drug addiction, or other underlying psychological issues.

The Toilet Paper Torch is a strange case of arson that occurred during a time of global crisis. It serves as a reminder of the strange and unpredictable ways in which people can act when faced with difficult circumstances. The incident also highlights the importance of understanding the motives behind arson and addressing the underlying issues that may lead someone to commit such a crime. While the shortage of toilet paper may have been a contributing factor in this case, it was ultimately the perpetrator's own psychological issues that led to his actions.

The Cat Arsonist

Arsonists often start fires for different reasons, from revenge to financial gain. But the Cat Arsonist, one of the most disturbing arsonists in history, had a different motive. This person's fascination with fire and cats led to a string of arson attacks that killed hundreds of felines and caused thousands of dollars in property damage.

The Cat Arsonist's reign of terror began in 1995 in San Jose, California. At first, the fires were small and contained, often targeting abandoned buildings and dumpsters. But the arsonist soon escalated to setting fire to occupied homes and apartment buildings.

The Cat Arsonist's signature was a cat figurine left at the scene of each fire. The figurine represented the arsonist's obsession with felines, but it also served as a taunt to the authorities trying to catch them.

The Cat Arsonist was careful to cover their tracks, using accelerants that were difficult to trace and setting fires at random times to avoid being seen. But despite their efforts, investigators were able to piece together a profile of the suspect.

The profile revealed that the Cat Arsonist was likely a male in his 20s or 30s with a fascination with fire and an unhealthy obsession with cats. He was also likely to have a history of cruelty to animals and possibly suffered from a mental illness.

Despite the profile, the Cat Arsonist continued to elude capture, setting fires across California for several years. The authorities had no idea where or when the next attack would occur, leaving residents living in fear.

The Cat Arsonist's most notorious attack occurred on December 12, 1998, in San Francisco. The arsonist set fire to an apartment building, killing five people and injuring 18 others. The building was home to many cats, and most of them died in the blaze.

The Cat Arsonist's reign of terror came to an end in 2001, when a man named David Richard started a fire in an apartment complex in Redwood City, California. Richard was not the Cat Arsonist, but he was caught after the fire and confessed to setting a series of other fires in the area.

During his interrogation, Richard revealed that he knew the Cat Arsonist and even helped him set some of the fires. Richard claimed that the Cat Arsonist was a man named Marvallous Keene, a 26-year-old man who had a history of mental illness and a fascination with cats.

Keene was eventually arrested and charged with 28 counts of arson, including the fire that killed five people in San Francisco. He pleaded guilty to all charges and was sentenced to 63 years in prison.

The Cat Arsonist's reign of terror had finally come to an end, but the damage had been done. Hundreds of cats had been killed, and many families had lost their homes and possessions. The Cat Arsonist's twisted obsession with cats had caused immeasurable pain and suffering.

The Cat Arsonist's case is a reminder of the dangers of obsession and the devastating consequences of arson. While most arsonists may not have the same twisted fascination with cats, their actions can have similarly tragic results.

The Cat Arsonist's story is also a testament to the tireless work of investigators and law enforcement officials who worked for years to catch the culprit.

The Birthday Cake Burner

In 2015, a woman in New York was arrested for setting fire to her neighbor's apartment during a birthday party. Dubbed the "Birthday Cake Burner," the woman's strange and destructive behavior left many people baffled.

The incident took place in the Bronx, where the woman, identified as 42-year-old Sonia Vargas, lived in a building with several other families. According to witnesses, Vargas was attending a birthday party in the apartment next door to hers when she suddenly became agitated and began arguing with other guests.

As the argument escalated, Vargas allegedly poured gasoline on the floor of the apartment and lit it on fire, causing the building to fill with smoke and flames. Guests at the party quickly evacuated the building, but not before several people suffered injuries, including burns and smoke inhalation.

When firefighters arrived on the scene, they found Vargas still inside her apartment, where she had barricaded herself. They were able to break down the door and take her into custody. She was later charged with arson and reckless endangerment.

The motive behind Vargas' bizarre behavior remains unclear, but some reports suggest that she may have been experiencing mental health issues at the time of the incident. According to neighbors, Vargas had a history of erratic behavior and had previously been seen wandering around the building naked.

The Birthday Cake Burner is just one example of the strange and unpredictable nature of arson crimes. While most arsonists have specific motives for setting fires, such as revenge or insurance fraud, there are some who seem to act out of pure impulse or delusion.

One such case occurred in 2003, when a man in Pennsylvania set fire to a grocery store after becoming convinced that the store was part of a government conspiracy to control his mind. Another case involved a woman in Texas who set fire to her home after believing that it was possessed by demons.

Arson crimes can have devastating consequences, both for the individuals involved and for the community at large. In addition to causing physical harm and property damage, arson fires can also lead to emotional trauma and financial losses.

To combat this type of crime, law enforcement agencies have developed specialized units that investigate and prevent arson. These units work closely with fire departments, insurance companies, and other organizations to identify potential arsonists and gather evidence that can be used to prosecute them.

Despite these efforts, arson remains a difficult crime to prevent and detect. In many cases, arsonists are able to cover their tracks by using accelerants or other methods to create misleading evidence.

The Birthday Cake Burner and other oddball arsonists serve as a reminder of the need for continued vigilance and awareness when it comes to preventing and solving arson crimes. By working together and staying alert, we can help keep our communities safe and secure from this destructive and unpredictable crime.

The Gas Station Arsonist

In 2016, a series of arson attacks occurred in Marion County, Florida. These attacks were targeted at gas stations, and authorities soon realized that they were dealing with a serial arsonist. The man responsible for these attacks was later identified as 46-year-old James Wayne Crain.

Crain's modus operandi was consistent throughout all of the arson attacks. He would approach a gas station, pour gasoline around the pumps, and then set it alight. The fires would quickly spread, causing significant damage to the gas station and posing a threat to nearby buildings and people. Thankfully, no one was injured during these attacks, but the potential for harm was very real.

Police were initially baffled as to the motivation behind these attacks. There didn't seem to be any clear reason why someone would target gas stations in this way. However, after conducting an investigation, they were able to link Crain to the crimes. He was eventually arrested and charged with multiple counts of arson.

During his trial, it was revealed that Crain had been struggling with mental health issues for some time. He had a history of drug abuse and had been diagnosed with bipolar disorder. He claimed that he didn't remember committing the arson attacks and that he was under the influence of drugs at the time. However, the evidence against him was overwhelming, and he was found guilty on all counts.

Crain was sentenced to 30 years in prison for his crimes. The judge in the case cited the potential danger that these attacks posed to the public and the need to send a strong message that such behavior would not be tolerated.

The Gas Station Arsonist case is a reminder of the danger posed by arson attacks. Not only do these attacks cause significant damage to property, but they can also put people's lives at risk. In this case, the authorities were fortunate to catch the perpetrator before anyone was hurt. However, this isn't always the case, and the consequences of such attacks can be devastating.

Arson investigations are notoriously difficult, as there is often little physical evidence to go on. In the Gas Station Arsonist case, police were able to use surveillance footage to identify the perpetrator. However, in many cases, arsonists are able to cover their tracks, making it very difficult to catch them.

The Gas Station Arsonist case also highlights the importance of mental health treatment. It's clear that Crain was struggling with mental health issues, and this likely contributed to his decision to commit these crimes. If he had received the help he needed earlier, perhaps these attacks could have been prevented.

Arson is a serious crime that can have far-reaching consequences. It's not just the damage to property that's at stake, but people's lives as well. The Gas Station Arsonist case is a reminder of the importance of vigilance and the need to take action when suspicious behavior is observed. It also highlights the need for better mental health care, as addressing underlying issues can help prevent these types of crimes from occurring in the first place.

The Gas Station Arsonist case is a cautionary tale about the dangers of arson and the importance of taking these crimes seriously. It's also a reminder that there are often complex factors at play in these cases, and that addressing these underlying issues is key to preventing future crimes.

The Fireworks Fiend

In 2017, a string of fires began to erupt in Southern California, leaving residents on edge and firefighters working tirelessly to contain them. But one particular fire stood out as particularly bizarre – it was started by a man who became known as the "Fireworks Fiend."

The Fireworks Fiend's first arson occurred on July 22, 2017, when he set fire to a hillside in the city of Fontana using illegal fireworks. Over the next several weeks, he continued to start fires in various locations throughout the region, including near the city of Highland, where a brush fire burned more than 200 acres and threatened homes.

Despite an intensive investigation by local law enforcement, the Fireworks Fiend continued to elude capture. However, on August 7, he struck again in the city of Yucaipa, where he set fire to a field and fled the scene. This time, however, a witness was able to provide a description of the suspect's vehicle.

Using this information, police were able to identify the vehicle and track down the Fireworks Fiend, whose real name was David Lawless. Lawless was a 38-year-old man who had a long history of drug abuse and criminal activity.

When police searched Lawless's home, they found a large stash of illegal fireworks, as well as evidence linking him to the various arson fires that had been plaguing the area. Lawless was arrested and charged with multiple counts of arson.

During his trial, Lawless claimed that he had set the fires in order to "blow off steam" and because he enjoyed watching the chaos that they caused. He also admitted to being a heavy drug user and said that he was under the influence of drugs during many of the arson incidents.

Despite his claims, Lawless was found guilty of all charges and sentenced to 15 years in prison. His crimes caused millions of dollars in damages and put many lives at risk, including those of firefighters who worked tirelessly to contain the blazes.

The Fireworks Fiend's reign of terror may have been short-lived, but his impact was felt throughout Southern California for months after his arrest. Many residents were left shaken by the string of fires and the knowledge that someone was deliberately setting them.

The Fireworks Fiend's case is a reminder of the destructive power of arson and the impact that a single individual can have on a community. It also serves as a cautionary tale about the dangers of illegal fireworks and the importance of responsible use.

While the Fireworks Fiend's motivations may have been rooted in drug abuse and a desire for chaos, his actions had very real and devastating consequences. The damage he caused will take years to repair, and the trauma that he inflicted on those who witnessed the fires will last even longer.

In the end, the Fireworks Fiend was brought to justice, but the scars of his crimes will continue to be felt in Southern California for many years to come.

The DIY Demolition

In 2018, a man in Michigan became known as the "DIY Demolition" after he set fire to his own house in an attempt to demolish it himself. The man, who was in his 80s, had grown tired of his house and decided that he wanted to tear it down and build a new one in its place.

Instead of hiring a professional demolition crew, the man decided to take matters into his own hands. He gathered a large quantity of fireworks, gasoline, and other flammable materials and placed them throughout his house. He then ignited the fireworks and fled the scene, hoping that the resulting fire would destroy the house and clear the way for his new construction project.

However, things did not go as planned. The fire quickly spread out of control and engulfed neighboring houses as well. The local fire department was called to the scene, but by the time they arrived, the fire had spread too far for them to be able to save the house or any of the neighboring properties.

The DIY Demolition caused an estimated $1.5 million in damages, and the man was charged with multiple counts of arson and reckless endangerment. He later pleaded guilty to the charges and was sentenced to serve time in prison.

The case of the DIY Demolition is a cautionary tale of the dangers of taking on complex projects without proper training or equipment. In addition to the damage caused to his own property, the man's actions put the lives of his neighbors and first responders at risk.

Arson is a serious crime that can have devastating consequences. It not only causes property damage and financial loss, but it can also lead to injury or death. The motives behind arson can vary widely, from financial gain to revenge to a desire for attention.

In some cases, arsonists are motivated by mental illness or emotional distress. They may feel a sense of power or control over their surroundings by setting fires, or they may be seeking help or attention in a misguided way. However, regardless of the motive, arson is always a dangerous and destructive act.

The DIY Demolition serves as a reminder that demolition and construction projects should always be left to the professionals. Attempting to take on these types of projects without the proper knowledge, training, and equipment can have serious consequences, not just for the person attempting the project but for those around them as well.

In addition, it highlights the importance of understanding the risks and consequences of arson. It is not a victimless crime, and those who commit it will be held accountable for their actions.

The case also illustrates the importance of prompt and effective response by first responders in the event of an arson. Firefighters and other emergency personnel put their lives on the line every day to protect their communities from the dangers of fire and other disasters. It is essential that they have the resources and support they need to do their jobs safely and effectively.

Ultimately, the story of the DIY Demolition is a cautionary tale about the dangers of taking on projects beyond one's capabilities and the serious consequences of arson. It is a reminder that there are always safer and more responsible ways to achieve one's goals, and that the safety and well-being of others should always be a top priority.

The Flame-Thrower Arsonist

In 2019, a bizarre arson case shocked Australia when a man armed with a flamethrower targeted multiple buildings in the city of Darwin. The suspect, identified as Ben Hoffmann, set fire to several buildings, including a pub and a political office, causing significant damage.

The attacks began in the early hours of June 14, when the 45-year-old Hoffmann broke into the Coopers Alehouse in the city's central business district. He sprayed the establishment with fuel and ignited it with his flamethrower, causing extensive damage to the building. Fortunately, no one was inside at the time, and the fire was quickly contained by firefighters.

Over the next few hours, Hoffmann continued his rampage, setting fire to at least three more buildings in the city. One of the buildings targeted was a nearby political office belonging to the Country Liberal Party, which was completely destroyed in the blaze. A nearby motel and an apartment complex were also targeted, but the fires were quickly extinguished before they could cause significant damage.

Despite the destructive nature of the attacks, no one was injured in the incidents. Police later apprehended Hoffmann and charged him with a range of offenses, including arson, property damage, and carrying an offensive weapon.

According to reports, Hoffmann had been living in Darwin for several months before the attacks and had no known connections to any of the targeted buildings. The motive for the arson spree remains unclear, with investigators stating that the suspect had not provided a coherent explanation for his actions.

However, it was later revealed that Hoffmann had a history of mental illness and drug addiction. In the days leading up to the attacks, he had reportedly been using the drug methamphetamine and had been exhibiting erratic and paranoid behavior.

The flamethrower used by Hoffmann was not a commercially available product, but rather a homemade device consisting of a pressurized fuel canister and a nozzle that sprayed a stream of ignited fuel. The device was highly dangerous and illegal, and its possession and use are strictly prohibited in Australia.

The incident prompted a significant public outcry, with many questioning how Hoffmann was able to acquire such a dangerous weapon in the first place. The incident also raised concerns about the prevalence of methamphetamine use in Australia and the impact it has on individuals with mental health issues.

The case of the flame-thrower arsonist is a stark reminder of the danger posed by individuals with untreated mental illness and drug addiction. It also highlights the need for stricter regulations on the possession and use of dangerous weapons, such as homemade flamethrowers.

The incident caused significant damage to the affected buildings, with some of them being completely destroyed in the fires. It also disrupted the lives of many people in the city of Darwin, causing fear and anxiety among local residents.

The case of the flame-thrower arsonist is a chilling reminder of the destructive power of fire and the dangers posed by individuals with untreated mental illness and drug addiction. The incident shocked the nation and prompted a renewed discussion on the need for stricter regulations on the possession and use of dangerous weapons.

The Church Burner

In 2020, a string of church fires plagued the state of Louisiana. The FBI, Louisiana State Fire Marshal's Office, and other law enforcement agencies worked tirelessly to investigate the cause of the fires and catch the culprit. It was soon discovered that the fires were the work of one man, Holden Matthews, who would come to be known as the Church Burner.

Matthews was a 21-year-old white male and the son of a local sheriff's deputy. He had grown up in the area and was known to be a talented musician who played in a local black metal band. However, his interest in this music genre would later become a key factor in the investigation of the church fires.

Between March and April of 2020, three historically black churches were burned down in St. Landry Parish, Louisiana. The first fire occurred on March 26th at the St. Mary Baptist Church in Port Barre, followed by the Greater Union Baptist Church in Opelousas on April 2nd, and then the Mount Pleasant Baptist Church in Opelousas on April 4th. The fires caused significant damage to the churches, with some of them being completely destroyed.

Investigators quickly identified similarities in the fires and suspected that they were connected. Evidence was collected from the crime scenes, including video footage from security cameras that showed a figure approaching the churches and setting them on fire.

Matthews was arrested on April 10th, 2020, and charged with three counts of arson. The FBI and other agencies had been monitoring him since the first fire and were able to track his movements through cell phone data and other means. When Matthews was apprehended, he was found with gas cans and a lighter in his possession, confirming suspicions that he was the Church Burner.

During his trial, it was revealed that Matthews had targeted the churches because of their historic significance to the black community. He reportedly held racist beliefs and had even mentioned his desire to start a race war. However, he also claimed to have set the fires as a means of gaining notoriety for his band.

Matthews eventually pleaded guilty to three counts of arson and one count of using fire to commit a federal felony. He was sentenced to 25 years in prison without the possibility of parole. His actions had caused significant harm to the churches and their congregations, as well as to the wider community who felt the impact of the hate crime.

The Church Burner's case is not an isolated one. Throughout history, churches and other places of worship have been targeted by arsonists for various reasons, including religious and political motives. In the United States, there have been several notable cases of church arson, including the 1996 series of fires in Alabama that resulted in the convictions of three members of the Ku Klux Klan.

Arson is a serious crime that can have devastating consequences. It not only destroys property but can also lead to loss of life and significant emotional trauma for those affected. The Church Burner's actions not only caused physical damage to the churches but also emotional harm to the congregations who had lost their places of worship and felt targeted by the perpetrator's racist beliefs.

The case also highlights the important role of law enforcement in investigating and solving crimes, particularly those that may have a hate crime element. Through the efforts of the FBI and other agencies, the Church Burner was apprehended and brought to justice, sending a message that such acts of hate and violence will not be tolerated in society.

The Hot Sauce Hellion

In 2021, a spicy incident took place in a small town in Texas that left locals and law enforcement scratching their heads. The culprit behind the strange arson was dubbed "The Hot Sauce Hellion" due to the fiery ingredient used in the crime.

The story began when a popular local restaurant, known for its signature hot sauce, was set ablaze in the early hours of the morning. The fire was contained to the kitchen area, but the damage was significant enough to force the business to close temporarily for repairs. Fortunately, no one was hurt in the incident, but investigators quickly determined that the fire was no accident.

As authorities began to investigate the arson, they found a strange note left at the scene of the crime. The note was written in bold red letters and read, "This is just the beginning. Your hot sauce is too hot to handle. -The Hot Sauce Hellion."

Residents in the small town were baffled by the strange message, and social media quickly lit up with speculation and theories about who could be behind the bizarre arson. Some people believed it was a disgruntled employee seeking revenge, while others thought it was a rival restaurant owner trying to eliminate the competition.

Despite the initial confusion, investigators soon made a breakthrough in the case when a witness came forward with information about a man who had been acting suspiciously around the restaurant on the night of the fire. The witness reported seeing a man with a large backpack lurking around the back entrance of the restaurant shortly before the fire was started.

With this information in hand, the police were able to track down the suspect, a man in his early 30s who lived in the town. The man was known to police for minor offenses, but he had no criminal history of arson or other violent crimes.

When the man was questioned by police, he initially denied any involvement in the fire. However, when presented with the evidence against him, he eventually confessed to the crime.

According to the suspect, he had been a regular customer at the restaurant for years, but he had always found the hot sauce to be too spicy for his taste. One day, he decided he had had enough and went to the restaurant to confront the owner about the sauce. When the owner refused to change the recipe, the suspect became enraged and decided to take matters into his own hands.

The man admitted to breaking into the restaurant after hours and pouring gallons of gasoline on the kitchen floor. He then used a lighter to start the fire and left the note as a warning to the owner.

The suspect was charged with arson and faced significant jail time for his actions. Many in the town were left shocked and saddened by the incident, and the once-beloved restaurant struggled to recover from the damage caused by the Hot Sauce Hellion.

The story of the Hot Sauce Hellion is a cautionary tale about the dangers of obsession and anger. What started as a disagreement over a condiment escalated into a dangerous act of arson that could have resulted in tragedy. It serves as a reminder that even the smallest things can have big consequences and that rational thinking should always prevail in situations of conflict.

The Hot Sauce Hellion may have thought he was making a statement, but instead, he only succeeded in causing harm to a community and damaging his own life in the process.

Weird White-Collar Crimes

The Caviar Crook

In 2012, a man in California made headlines for his unusual crime - stealing more than $100,000 worth of caviar from a distribution company. This is the story of the Caviar Crook.

The man in question was 42-year-old Nicky Paul Alexander, who had been working as a truck driver for a caviar distribution company in Petaluma, California for about a year. One day, he decided to take matters into his own hands and steal a truckload of caviar.

Alexander was able to successfully pull off the heist by using his knowledge of the company's security protocols. He disabled the security cameras and alarms and was able to load up a truck with over 100 cases of caviar, worth around $100,000.

However, Alexander's luck didn't last long. The company quickly realized that a significant amount of caviar was missing and reported the theft to the police. Investigators were able to identify Alexander as the suspect based on evidence found at the scene and through witness interviews.

Alexander was arrested and charged with grand theft, burglary, and conspiracy to commit a crime. He ultimately pleaded guilty and was sentenced to three years in prison.

What motivated Alexander to steal such a large quantity of caviar? It's unclear, but some speculate that he may have been trying to start his own caviar distribution business or simply wanted to sell the stolen goods for a profit.

The Caviar Crook's crime may seem comical at first, but the consequences of his actions were serious. Caviar is a luxury food item that is often associated with high-end restaurants and events, and stealing such a large amount had a significant impact on the company's finances and reputation.

This incident also sheds light on the prevalence of white-collar crime in the United States. While street crimes like robbery and burglary often make the headlines, white-collar crimes like embezzlement, fraud, and insider trading are just as common and often more damaging.

In fact, white-collar crimes cost the United States billions of dollars each year and can have a devastating impact on individuals, businesses, and the economy as a whole. These crimes often involve individuals in positions of power or trust, who use their influence to commit fraudulent or illegal activities for personal gain.

The case of the Caviar Crook serves as a reminder that no one is immune to the temptation of financial gain, and that even seemingly harmless crimes can have serious consequences. It also highlights the importance of strong security measures and regular monitoring of financial transactions, to prevent these types of crimes from happening in the first place.

The story of the Caviar Crook may seem like a strange and amusing crime, but it is a reminder of the prevalence and impact of white-collar crime. Alexander's actions not only resulted in his own imprisonment but also caused significant financial and reputational damage to the caviar distribution company. This story serves as a warning that even those in positions of trust can be tempted by the lure of financial gain, and that vigilance and strong security measures are essential to prevent these types of crimes.

The Trash-Talking Trader

The world of finance and trading has long been associated with high-stakes deals, fast-paced action, and cut-throat competition. However, in 2013, one former trader took things to a new level when he began sending anonymous emails filled with insults and threats to his former colleagues. This bizarre case came to be known as the "Trash-Talking Trader" scandal and quickly became the talk of the financial industry.

The man at the center of the scandal was a former employee of a prominent trading firm in New York City. According to reports, he had been fired from his job due to poor performance and a bad attitude. However, instead of accepting his termination and moving on, the disgruntled trader decided to take revenge on his former colleagues in a most unusual way.

Using a fake email account, the trader began sending anonymous messages to his former coworkers, filled with insults, expletives, and even death threats. The messages were often crude and insulting, attacking the recipients' intelligence, appearance, and professional skills. At first, many of the recipients dismissed the emails as childish pranks or the work of a disgruntled ex-employee. However, as the messages continued, their tone became increasingly menacing and threatening.

Some of the messages contained explicit references to violence, including threats to physically harm the recipients or their families. One message, in particular, caused alarm when it mentioned a specific date and time and warned of a "bloodbath" to come. The recipients were understandably shaken by these threats, and many of them contacted the police.

After a lengthy investigation, the police were able to trace the emails back to the former trader. He was arrested and charged with a variety of offenses, including harassment, stalking, and making terroristic threats. The trader initially denied any involvement in the emails, but he was eventually forced to admit to the crime when the evidence against him became overwhelming.

In court, the trader's behavior continued to be bizarre and erratic. He frequently interrupted the proceedings with outbursts and insults, earning himself numerous reprimands from the judge. At one point, he even accused his defense attorney of being in cahoots with the prosecutors. Despite his erratic behavior, the trader was found guilty of all charges and was sentenced to two years in prison.

The Trash-Talking Trader scandal was a wake-up call for the financial industry, highlighting the dangers of workplace harassment and the need for stronger measures to protect employees from such behavior. The incident also underscored the importance of monitoring employees' online activities and the potential risks posed by social media and other digital platforms.

The case also shed light on the psychology of revenge and the dangers of toxic workplace environments. According to experts, the trader's behavior was likely driven by a deep-seated sense of anger and resentment towards his former colleagues, combined with a desire for revenge. His inability to accept responsibility for his poor performance and his subsequent firing only fueled his resentment, leading him to lash out in a most destructive way.

The Trash-Talking Trader scandal also had wider implications for the financial industry, which was already grappling with issues of corruption, fraud, and insider trading. The incident further damaged the industry's reputation and led to calls for greater transparency and accountability. The scandal served as a stark reminder that unethical behavior can have serious consequences, both for the individuals involved and for the industry as a whole.

The Naked Trader

In 2014, a former investment banker in Hong Kong made headlines after being arrested for running through the streets completely naked. The incident was a bizarre reaction to the man's financial losses on a single stock trade.

The man, whose name has not been publicly released, was a former employee of the investment bank BNP Paribas. He had reportedly invested a large amount of his personal savings in the stock of a Chinese company, hoping to make a profit. However, the stock price took a sharp turn for the worse, and the man lost a significant amount of money.

The loss apparently sent the former banker into a state of extreme distress, and he decided to take to the streets in a state of complete undress. According to eyewitness reports, he ran through the busy Central district of Hong Kong, shouting and gesticulating wildly.

Police officers quickly arrived on the scene and arrested the naked trader. He was taken into custody and charged with indecent exposure and disorderly conduct. After spending several days in jail, he was released on bail pending trial.

The incident quickly became a media sensation, with news outlets around the world reporting on the bizarre incident. Many observers speculated that the man may have been suffering from a mental health condition, or that he may have been under the influence of drugs or alcohol.

However, others pointed to the high-pressure environment of the financial industry as a possible cause of the man's breakdown. Investment banking and trading are notoriously stressful professions, and many individuals in these fields are known to work long hours and take on significant amounts of risk.

In the aftermath of the incident, the man's former employer, BNP Paribas, released a statement expressing its concern for the man's well-being. The company also emphasized that the man had not been working for the bank at the time of the incident, and that his behavior was in no way reflective of the company's values.

The naked trader's trial was held several months later, and he was found guilty of the charges against him. He was sentenced to several weeks in jail and ordered to pay a fine. After serving his sentence, he reportedly left Hong Kong and returned to his home country.

The incident has since become something of a cautionary tale for investors and traders in the financial industry. It serves as a reminder that even the most successful and experienced professionals can experience significant financial losses, and that it is important to maintain a healthy perspective on money and investments.

Moreover, the incident highlights the importance of mental health awareness and support in high-stress industries like finance. Many companies in the financial sector have implemented employee wellness programs and other initiatives aimed at promoting mental health and well-being.

The naked trader's story is a bizarre and somewhat tragic example of the pressures and risks associated with high-stakes financial trading. While his actions may have been extreme, they serve as a reminder that financial success can be fleeting, and that it is important to maintain a balanced and healthy approach to money and investments.

The Wine-Sipping Swindler

In 2015, a woman in Oregon made headlines after being arrested for stealing over $1 million worth of wine from a wealthy collector. The perpetrator, Andrea Joy Kreamer, was an experienced wine aficionado and used her knowledge to gain the trust of her victim.

Kreamer met the wine collector through a mutual friend, and the two quickly bonded over their shared love of wine. She even worked for the collector for a brief period, giving her the opportunity to learn about the wine cellar's layout and security systems.

Kreamer's scheme began in 2012 when she started to steal bottles of wine from the collector's cellar. She initially took just a few bottles at a time, but as time went on, her thefts became bolder and more frequent. Kreamer's criminal activities went unnoticed until 2013 when the collector began to notice that his prized collection was dwindling.

The collector installed security cameras in his cellar, hoping to catch the thief in action. But Kreamer was careful and never appeared on camera. Eventually, the collector became suspicious of Kreamer, and the police were called in to investigate.

The investigation revealed that Kreamer had stolen over 5,000 bottles of wine from the collector's cellar, with a total estimated value of over $1 million. Kreamer had even created a fake wine cellar in her own home, where she stored the stolen bottles.

Kreamer's downfall came when she attempted to sell some of the stolen wine to a local restaurant. The restaurant owner became suspicious of the low price and contacted the wine collector, who then contacted the police. Kreamer was arrested and charged with theft and money laundering.

During her trial, Kreamer claimed that she had a drinking problem and was trying to fund her addiction. She also stated that she had intended to pay the collector back for the stolen wine. However, the jury did not believe her and found her guilty on all charges.

Kreamer was sentenced to 7 years in prison, and she was also ordered to pay $1.2 million in restitution to the wine collector. The case gained widespread media attention, with many people shocked that someone could steal so much wine without being caught for such a long time.

The case also highlighted the value of wine as an investment and the importance of proper security measures. Wine theft is a growing problem around the world, with high-value wine collections becoming targets for criminals.

In 2019, a wine collector in France was robbed of over $300,000 worth of wine, with thieves making off with 168 bottles of rare and expensive wine. The theft prompted authorities to issue warnings to wine collectors to take extra precautions to protect their valuable collections.

The Wine-Sipping Swindler case serves as a reminder of the dangers of placing trust in others, particularly when it comes to valuable possessions. It also highlights the importance of strong security measures, particularly when it comes to wine collections and other valuable assets.

The case of the Wine-Sipping Swindler shows how a seemingly harmless hobby or passion can turn into a criminal enterprise. Kreamer's love for wine led her down a path of theft and deception, ultimately resulting in her arrest and imprisonment. The case also highlights the need for vigilance and caution when dealing with high-value items, particularly when others are involved.

The Email Impersonator

In 2016, a man in California was charged with impersonating his boss via email and directing company funds to his personal bank account. The man, whose name was not disclosed, worked for a financial services company and had access to the company's email system.

Using his knowledge of his boss's writing style and email habits, the man created a fake email address that closely resembled his boss's and began sending emails to the company's accounting department. The emails instructed the department to wire funds to a bank account that the man had set up in his own name.

Initially, the scheme worked. The man was able to redirect thousands of dollars from the company's accounts into his personal bank account without raising suspicion. However, his luck eventually ran out.

The real boss of the company noticed discrepancies in the company's financial records and began investigating. It didn't take long for him to realize that someone had been impersonating him via email. The boss immediately contacted law enforcement, who launched an investigation.

Through their investigation, law enforcement was able to trace the bank account that the funds had been wired to back to the man. They also discovered that the man had used the money to fund an extravagant lifestyle, including purchasing a new car and taking vacations.

The man was arrested and charged with multiple counts of fraud, identity theft, and computer-related crimes. He eventually pled guilty to the charges and was sentenced to several years in prison.

This case highlights the dangers of cybercrime and the importance of maintaining strong security measures when it comes to email and other online accounts. It also serves as a reminder that even those who work in the financial industry can be susceptible to committing fraud.

Many companies have since implemented additional security measures to prevent similar incidents from happening in the future. This includes things like two-factor authentication for email accounts, regular security audits, and increased employee training on how to recognize and report fraudulent activity.

It's important for both companies and individuals to take steps to protect themselves from cybercrime. This includes things like using strong passwords, avoiding clicking on suspicious links or attachments in emails, and keeping antivirus and anti-malware software up to date.

In addition, individuals should be careful about sharing personal information online and should always be suspicious of any unsolicited emails or phone calls asking for sensitive information.

The case of the email impersonator serves as a cautionary tale about the dangers of cybercrime and the importance of maintaining strong security measures to protect against it. While the man in this case may have thought he could get away with his scheme, he eventually faced the consequences of his actions and learned the hard way that crime doesn't pay.

The Library Looters

In 2017, a husband and wife duo in Utah made headlines when they were arrested for a string of library thefts that had taken place over several years. The couple, John and Julie, had stolen over 2,000 rare books and manuscripts from libraries across the United States. Their haul was estimated to be worth over $1.5 million.

John and Julie's modus operandi was simple yet effective. They would visit libraries under the guise of researchers, making detailed notes of the books and manuscripts they were interested in. They would then return to the library at a later time and steal the items, often hiding them in specially designed bags.

Their thefts were not limited to one type of library or a particular region. They targeted public libraries, university libraries, and museums across the country, including the University of Vermont, the Carnegie Library of Pittsburgh, and the Boston Public Library.

Their scheme was finally uncovered in 2017, when an employee at the Carnegie Library of Pittsburgh noticed that several rare books were missing. An investigation led to the discovery of John and Julie's storage unit, where they had been keeping their stolen goods. The couple was arrested and charged with theft, conspiracy, and interstate transportation of stolen property.

The library thefts shocked the nation, not only for the scale of the crime but also for the rarity and historical significance of the stolen items. Among the stolen items were a 1566 copy of Copernicus' "De Revolutionibus Orbium Coelestium," a 1632 edition of Galileo's "Dialogue Concerning the Two Chief World Systems," and a first edition of Isaac Newton's "Philosophiae Naturalis Principia Mathematica."

It soon emerged that John and Julie had been selling the stolen items on the black market for years, using aliases and fake identities to avoid detection. The couple had made a significant profit from their crimes, but the stolen items were often damaged or destroyed in the process.

The case of the library looters raised questions about the security of libraries and the value we place on cultural heritage. It highlighted the need for increased vigilance and security measures in libraries across the country.

In the aftermath of the thefts, many libraries reviewed and improved their security protocols. The Boston Public Library, for example, installed new alarm systems and added more security personnel to its staff. Other libraries began to require researchers to provide identification and background information before being granted access to rare and valuable items.

The case also served as a cautionary tale about the dangers of greed and obsession. John and Julie had become so fixated on acquiring rare books and manuscripts that they had lost sight of the value of these items beyond their monetary worth. They had risked their freedom and their reputation in pursuit of their obsession.

John and Julie pleaded guilty to the charges against them and were sentenced to prison. The stolen items were returned to their rightful owners, but many of them had been damaged beyond repair. The case of the library looters remains a reminder of the importance of preserving cultural heritage and the need for continued vigilance and security measures to protect it.

The Credit Card Collector

White-collar crimes come in many different forms and can involve individuals from all walks of life. In 2018, a man in New Jersey made headlines when he was arrested for stealing credit card numbers and using them to purchase collectible sports memorabilia.

The man, whose name was not disclosed in media reports, had been collecting sports memorabilia for many years and had a particular interest in autographed items. However, his passion for collecting became an addiction, and he began using stolen credit card numbers to purchase items online.

The man was able to obtain the credit card numbers by hacking into various websites and stealing the information. He would then use the stolen credit card numbers to purchase collectible sports memorabilia from online dealers. Once he had received the items, he would sell them to other collectors for a profit.

The man's scheme came to light when a suspicious sports memorabilia dealer contacted the authorities. The dealer had received a large order for several expensive items, and the credit card used to make the purchase was flagged as suspicious. When the authorities investigated, they found that the credit card had been stolen and used to make several other purchases of sports memorabilia.

After a thorough investigation, the man was arrested and charged with multiple counts of fraud and identity theft. He pled guilty to the charges and was sentenced to several years in prison.

This case highlights the dangers of online fraud and the importance of protecting personal information. The man was able to obtain credit card numbers by hacking into websites and stealing the information. Consumers should take precautions to protect their personal information, such as using strong passwords and avoiding using the same password for multiple accounts.

It also shows how easy it can be for someone to become addicted to collecting and how that addiction can lead to criminal behavior. The man's passion for collecting sports memorabilia led him to commit fraud and identity theft, which ultimately landed him in prison.

The case of the credit card collector serves as a reminder of the importance of being vigilant when it comes to online security and the risks associated with addiction. White-collar crimes can have serious consequences, both for the individuals involved and for society as a whole. It is up to all of us to take steps to prevent these crimes from happening and to hold those who commit them accountable for their actions.

The Imposter CEO Scam

The Imposter CEO Scam is a sophisticated form of white-collar crime that has become increasingly common in recent years. It involves an individual posing as a high-ranking executive of a company and tricking employees into transferring large sums of money into their account.

In 2020, a man in Germany was arrested for perpetrating such a scam. He had managed to convince an employee of a multinational company that he was the CEO, using a combination of social engineering tactics and fake emails. The employee then transferred over $1 million to the scammer's account, thinking that they were following the CEO's orders.

The scammer had spent months carefully researching the company and its executives, as well as the employee he planned to target. He created fake email addresses that closely resembled those of the CEO and other high-ranking executives, and used them to communicate with the employee.

The emails were written in a convincing tone and contained specific details about the company's operations and plans, which helped to build the employee's trust in the scammer. The scammer also used psychological manipulation techniques, such as fear and urgency, to pressure the employee into transferring the money.

The employee eventually became suspicious and contacted the company's actual CEO, who informed them that they had been scammed. The company then reported the incident to the authorities, who were able to track down the scammer and arrest him.

This type of scam is often successful because it preys on human vulnerabilities such as trust, fear, and the desire to please one's superiors. Employees may also be more likely to comply with a request from a high-ranking executive, especially if they feel that it is urgent or important.

To prevent such scams from occurring, companies need to be vigilant about their cybersecurity measures and train their employees to recognize and report suspicious emails. They should also establish clear protocols for authorizing financial transactions and verify all requests from high-ranking executives before transferring funds.

The consequences of falling victim to an imposter CEO scam can be severe for both the employee and the company. In addition to financial losses, the company's reputation and customer trust can be damaged, and the employee may face disciplinary action or even legal consequences.

In this case, the German authorities were able to recover some of the money that had been transferred to the scammer's account, but it is likely that the victim company suffered significant losses as a result of the scam.

The Imposter CEO Scam is just one example of the types of white-collar crimes that can be perpetrated using technology and social engineering tactics. As more companies move their operations online and rely on digital communication, the risk of such crimes is likely to increase.

Therefore, it is essential for companies to be proactive in their cybersecurity measures and for individuals to be vigilant about protecting their personal and financial information online. Only by staying informed and taking proactive steps can we hope to prevent white-collar crimes like the Imposter CEO Scam from occurring in the future.

The Chocolate Con Artist

In 2020, a man in England made headlines for a bizarre white-collar crime: stealing over 20,000 chocolate bars from the factory where he worked. The man, identified as Neale Homer, worked at the Barry Callebaut chocolate factory in Banbury, Oxfordshire, where he had access to large quantities of chocolate.

Over a period of several months, Homer stole thousands of chocolate bars from the factory, including popular brands such as Kit Kat, Crunchie, and Dairy Milk. He then sold the stolen chocolate on eBay and other online marketplaces, making a profit of over £27,000 ($37,000).

Homer's crime was eventually discovered when the factory's management noticed that large quantities of chocolate were missing from their inventory. They launched an investigation and discovered that Homer had been stealing chocolate bars by hiding them in his bag and coat as he left the factory.

When confronted by the police, Homer admitted to stealing the chocolate and selling it online. He was arrested and charged with theft and money laundering. In October 2020, he was sentenced to two years and six months in prison.

Homer's case was particularly unusual because of the sheer amount of chocolate he stole and the creative ways he found to sell it. While stealing from one's employer is unfortunately not uncommon, stealing chocolate bars and reselling them online is a particularly bizarre twist.

However, the case also highlights the serious nature of white-collar crime. While Homer's crime may seem trivial compared to other white-collar crimes, such as embezzlement or insider trading, it still resulted in significant financial losses for his employer and was a serious breach of trust.

Furthermore, white-collar crime often goes undetected or unpunished, as perpetrators may have access to resources and connections that allow them to evade justice. In Homer's case, it was only through the diligence of his employer's management and the authorities that he was caught and brought to justice.

It is also worth noting that white-collar crime can have serious consequences beyond financial losses. In some cases, it can cause long-lasting harm to individuals and communities, as seen in cases such as the Enron scandal or the 2008 financial crisis.

In the case of the chocolate con artist, Homer's crime may seem harmless in comparison. However, it still highlights the need for accountability and transparency in all forms of white-collar crime, no matter how unusual or seemingly insignificant.

The case of the chocolate con artist is a reminder that white-collar crime can take many forms, and that it can have serious consequences for both individuals and society as a whole. While it may seem like a victimless crime, the theft of thousands of chocolate bars is still a serious breach of trust and an illegal act that deserves punishment.

The Art Forgery Faker

Art forgery is a lucrative business, but it's also illegal. In 2021, a man in Spain was arrested for creating and selling fake paintings by famous artists. The man, who has not been identified, was caught after art experts noticed discrepancies in the paintings' styles and signatures.

According to authorities, the man had been selling the fake paintings for years, earning hundreds of thousands of euros in profits. He had managed to fool collectors and art dealers into believing that his paintings were authentic works by artists such as Pablo Picasso and Joan Miró.

The man was a skilled artist who had studied the styles and techniques of famous painters, allowing him to recreate their works with remarkable accuracy. He used a variety of materials, including vintage canvases and paint, to create convincing forgeries.

However, it was his attention to detail that ultimately led to his downfall. Experts noticed that the paintings he was selling had minor flaws, such as incorrect signatures or paint that had been applied too smoothly. These discrepancies were subtle, but they were enough to raise suspicions.

Once the authorities were alerted to the possible forgeries, they launched an investigation that eventually led to the man's arrest. He was charged with fraud and forgery, and faces a lengthy prison sentence if convicted.

The case highlights the lucrative and illegal world of art forgery. Forgeries have been around for centuries, with some of the most famous artists in history, including Vincent van Gogh and Rembrandt, falling victim to the practice. Forgers often try to replicate the styles of famous artists, or create completely new works that they pass off as undiscovered masterpieces.

The art world is a highly competitive and often secretive industry, making it an ideal breeding ground for forgers. Collectors and dealers are always on the lookout for rare and valuable pieces, which makes them vulnerable to scams and frauds.

To combat the problem, art experts have developed a range of techniques for identifying forgeries, including carbon dating and spectroscopy. These techniques allow experts to examine paintings in detail, looking for inconsistencies in the materials used and the techniques employed by the artist.

In addition, many countries have laws and regulations in place to protect against art fraud. For example, in the United States, the FBI's Art Crime Team investigates cases of art theft and fraud, while the federal government has laws in place to protect art and cultural property.

Despite these efforts, however, art forgery remains a persistent problem. The high prices commanded by authentic works of art make it an attractive target for fraudsters, who are often highly skilled at creating convincing fakes.

In the case of the Spanish man, his love of art and his desire for money led him down a dangerous path. His forgeries may have been convincing, but they ultimately proved to be his undoing. The case serves as a reminder of the dangers of art forgery, and the importance of protecting the integrity of the art world.

The case of the Spanish art forger demonstrates the ongoing problem of art fraud, and the importance of protecting the authenticity of works of art. The man's arrest is a reminder that forgeries can be convincing, but they can also be detected with the right techniques and expertise.

Eccentric Extortion

The Catnapper

In 2009, a man in California was arrested for a peculiar crime that left many pet owners in distress. Known as the "Catnapper," this man had a habit of stealing cats from their homes and then demanding ransom money from their owners in exchange for their safe return. This bizarre and unsettling crime spree went on for several months before authorities were finally able to catch the perpetrator.

The Catnapper's crimes were initially discovered by a group of concerned pet owners who had formed a Facebook group to discuss their missing cats. They soon realized that several of them had received strange phone calls from a man demanding large sums of money for the safe return of their pets. Some of the owners paid the ransom, but their cats were never returned.

The police were alerted to the situation, and they began investigating the mysterious cat kidnapper. They discovered that the man was targeting cats from affluent neighborhoods and using a variety of tactics to lure them out of their homes. He would leave out food or toys in order to entice the cats, and then snatch them up when they came close.

The Catnapper's downfall came when he tried to extort money from an undercover police officer who had posed as a cat owner. He was arrested and charged with several counts of extortion and theft. During the investigation, police found several cats in his possession, and many more were never recovered.

The Catnapper's motives for his crimes remain unclear, but some speculate that he may have had a psychological disorder that drove him to seek attention and control through these heinous acts. Others believe that he was simply after money and saw cats as an easy target. Whatever his motivations may have been, the Catnapper's crimes had a profound impact on the community and left many pet owners feeling vulnerable and afraid.

The incident shed light on the growing problem of pet theft in the United States. According to the American Kennel Club, an estimated 2 million pets are stolen each year, and only a small percentage of them are ever returned to their owners. Pet theft can be a lucrative business for criminals, who can sell animals on the black market or use them for dog fighting or other illegal activities.

In response to the Catnapper's crimes, many pet owners began taking extra precautions to protect their pets, such as installing security cameras or keeping them indoors. The incident also prompted lawmakers to consider tougher penalties for pet theft and to create a national pet theft database to help reunite lost pets with their owners.

The Catnapper's crimes were undoubtedly bizarre and unsettling, but they also served as a wake-up call for pet owners across the country. By raising awareness about the issue of pet theft and inspiring action to protect animals, this strange and troubling case may have ultimately done some good in the world.

The Virtual Kidnapper

In 2012, a new type of kidnapping started emerging in Mexico - virtual kidnapping. The criminals would use social media to target individuals and their families, tricking them into believing their loved ones had been kidnapped and demanding a ransom in exchange for their release.

The virtual kidnapping scheme involved the use of elaborate stories and sound effects to create a sense of urgency and fear in the victims. The criminals would often impersonate the kidnapped individual, making it seem like they were in danger and needed help. They would demand a ransom payment to be made through wire transfer or other untraceable methods, warning the victims not to involve the police or they would harm their loved ones.

The scheme was highly effective, and the virtual kidnappers were able to extort millions of dollars from their victims. They targeted anyone they thought they could exploit, from wealthy businessmen to middle-class families. The scheme was so successful that it spread beyond Mexico to other countries in Latin America and even to the United States.

The authorities soon caught on to the scheme and started warning the public about the dangers of virtual kidnapping. They advised people to be cautious about the information they shared on social media and to verify the whereabouts of their loved ones before sending any money. The authorities also launched investigations into the virtual kidnapping rings and arrested several individuals involved in the scheme.

One of the most high-profile arrests was that of a woman named Yanira Maldonado. In 2013, Maldonado and her husband were returning from a funeral in Mexico when they were stopped at a checkpoint. The police found 12 pounds of marijuana under their bus seat and arrested Maldonado, accusing her of drug smuggling. Maldonado denied the charges and claimed that she was a victim of virtual kidnapping. She said that she had received a call from someone claiming to be from the Mexican cartel and demanding a ransom for her release. She claimed that she had paid the ransom and was released, but the kidnappers had planted the drugs on her to cover up their tracks.

The case attracted widespread media attention, and Maldonado's supporters launched a social media campaign to free her. The authorities eventually dropped the drug charges against her, and she was released after spending more than a week in jail. Maldonado's case highlighted the dangers of virtual kidnapping and the need for better education and awareness about the scheme.

The virtual kidnapping scheme has continued to evolve over the years, with criminals finding new ways to exploit technology and social media to target their victims. The authorities have responded by increasing their efforts to track down and prosecute the virtual kidnappers. However, the scheme remains a significant threat in many parts of the world, and the public must remain vigilant and cautious.

The virtual kidnapping scheme is an example of an eccentric form of extortion that emerged in Mexico in 2012. The criminals used social media to trick people into believing their loved ones had been kidnapped and demanded ransom money in exchange for their release. The scheme was highly effective and spread beyond Mexico to other parts of Latin America and the United States. The authorities responded by warning the public about the dangers of virtual kidnapping and launching investigations into the virtual kidnapping rings. The scheme continues to be a threat, and the public must remain vigilant to avoid falling victim to it.

The Robotic Ransom

In 2014, a group of hackers in Australia executed a bizarre form of extortion that involved taking control of a factory's robotic equipment and demanding a ransom in exchange for halting the machines from causing destruction.

The attack, which took place in the state of Victoria, targeted a factory that used robotic arms to cut, shape, and assemble metal parts. The hackers infiltrated the factory's computer systems and gained control of the robotic equipment, causing it to malfunction and damage the products being produced.

The factory's owners received an email from the hackers, who demanded an undisclosed amount of Bitcoin in exchange for halting the robotic rampage. The email also contained a threat that the hackers would continue to cause destruction if the ransom was not paid.

The owners immediately contacted the police and shut down the factory to prevent further damage. The police launched an investigation and worked with cybersecurity experts to track down the hackers. The investigation revealed that the hackers had used a technique known as spear-phishing to gain access to the factory's computer systems.

Spear-phishing is a type of email scam that involves sending fraudulent emails that appear to be from a trusted source, such as a colleague or a supplier, in order to trick the recipient into revealing sensitive information or clicking on a malicious link. The hackers used spear-phishing to gain access to the factory's computer systems and install malware that allowed them to take control of the robotic equipment.

The police were able to trace the Bitcoin payment to an online account controlled by the hackers and arrested two men who were found to be responsible for the attack. The men were charged with extortion, conspiracy, and unauthorized access to a computer system, and faced up to 10 years in prison if convicted.

The incident highlighted the growing threat of cyber attacks and the need for companies to invest in cybersecurity measures to protect their computer systems and assets. It also demonstrated the potential for hackers to use technology to cause physical damage and disrupt operations, which poses a significant risk to businesses and critical infrastructure.

The case also shed light on the use of Bitcoin as a means of payment for ransom demands, as the cryptocurrency offers a high degree of anonymity and is difficult to trace. Bitcoin has become a popular choice for cybercriminals involved in extortion schemes, as it allows them to receive payment without revealing their identity or location.

In response to the incident, the Australian government launched a review of the country's cybersecurity policies and practices, with a focus on strengthening the nation's defenses against cyber attacks. The review recommended a range of measures, including increased investment in cybersecurity, better collaboration between government and industry, and the development of a national cybersecurity strategy.

The case of the robotic ransom highlights the need for businesses to be vigilant and proactive in their approach to cybersecurity. Companies must take steps to protect their computer systems and data from cyber attacks, including implementing strong passwords, regularly updating software, and training employees on how to recognize and avoid phishing scams.

The Celebrity Blackmailer

In 2015, a man in England was arrested for attempting to blackmail a well-known celebrity by threatening to release private videos. This high-profile case drew a lot of attention to the issue of celebrity privacy and the lengths some people will go to in order to exploit it.

The man in question, who cannot be named for legal reasons, was a former employee of the celebrity. He allegedly obtained access to private videos of the celebrity engaged in sexual activity and threatened to release them to the public if he was not paid a substantial sum of money.

The celebrity in question immediately contacted the police and the man was arrested shortly after. He was charged with blackmail and faced up to 14 years in prison if convicted.

The case shed light on the prevalence of celebrity blackmail in the age of social media and the internet. With the widespread availability of digital content and the ability to share it with a global audience in seconds, celebrities are often targeted by individuals seeking to exploit their private lives for financial gain.

In recent years, there have been a number of high-profile cases involving celebrity blackmail. In 2014, a man was arrested for attempting to blackmail a member of the British Royal Family by threatening to release embarrassing photographs. In 2016, a woman was arrested for blackmailing a well-known actor by threatening to reveal intimate photographs.

These cases demonstrate the dangers of fame in the modern world and the lengths some people will go to in order to exploit it. Celebrities are often the targets of blackmailers and extortionists, who seek to profit from their private lives and the secrets they keep hidden.

In response to the increasing prevalence of celebrity blackmail, many celebrities have taken steps to protect their privacy and safeguard their personal information. Some have employed teams of security experts to monitor their online activity and ensure that their personal information is kept secure. Others have taken legal action against those who attempt to exploit their privacy for financial gain.

Despite these efforts, however, the risk of celebrity blackmail remains a constant threat in the modern world. With the proliferation of social media and digital content, it has never been easier for individuals to gain access to private information and exploit it for personal gain.

The case of the celebrity blackmailer also highlights the importance of strong cybersecurity measures for individuals and organizations alike. The man in question was able to obtain access to the private videos through his position as a former employee of the celebrity. This underscores the need for organizations to implement robust security protocols and to carefully manage access to sensitive information.

Ultimately, the case of the celebrity blackmailer serves as a cautionary tale about the dangers of privacy in the digital age. While the ability to connect with others and share information has brought many benefits, it has also created new risks and vulnerabilities. Celebrities, in particular, must be vigilant about protecting their personal information and guarding against those who seek to exploit it for financial gain.

The case of the celebrity blackmailer in 2015 was a shocking reminder of the lengths some people will go to in order to exploit the private lives of others. It highlighted the risks and vulnerabilities associated with fame in the digital age and underscored the importance of strong cybersecurity measures for individuals and organizations alike.

The Bitcoin Bandit

In 2016, a group of hackers launched a widespread ransomware attack targeting victims across the United States. Dubbed the "Bitcoin Bandit," this group used a type of malware known as "Locky" to infect victims' computers and encrypt their files, making them inaccessible unless a ransom was paid in Bitcoin.

The Bitcoin Bandit's attacks were highly sophisticated and well-organized. They used a variety of methods to distribute the Locky malware, including spam emails and compromised websites. Once the malware was installed on a victim's computer, it would begin encrypting their files and display a message demanding a ransom payment in Bitcoin.

Victims were given a deadline to pay the ransom, after which the cost would increase or their files would be permanently deleted. The Bitcoin Bandit typically demanded between 1 and 2 Bitcoin, which at the time was worth several hundred dollars.

The attacks were highly effective, with many victims choosing to pay the ransom rather than risk losing their important files. The Bitcoin Bandit is believed to have earned millions of dollars through their ransomware attacks.

Law enforcement agencies across the United States worked tirelessly to track down the Bitcoin Bandit and bring them to justice. In 2017, two men were arrested and charged with conspiracy to commit computer fraud and extortion in connection with the attacks.

The two men, identified as Faramarz Shahi Savandi and Mohammad Mehdi Shah Mansouri, were Iranian nationals who had carried out the attacks from their home country. They were extradited to the United States to face trial.

During the trial, it was revealed that Savandi and Mansouri had targeted victims across a wide range of industries, including healthcare, education, and government. They had also used a variety of techniques to evade detection, including creating fake websites and using fake identities to register domain names.

Despite their efforts, however, law enforcement agencies were able to trace the Bitcoin Bandit's activities back to Savandi and Mansouri. In 2019, the two men were found guilty on multiple charges related to the ransomware attacks and were sentenced to prison.

The Bitcoin Bandit's attacks served as a wake-up call for individuals and organizations around the world to take cybersecurity seriously. As ransomware attacks become more common and more sophisticated, it's essential that people take steps to protect themselves and their data.

This includes keeping software and operating systems up-to-date, using strong passwords, and being cautious when opening emails or clicking on links from unknown sources. It's also a good idea to keep backups of important files in case they become encrypted by ransomware.

The Bitcoin Bandit's ransomware attacks were a highly effective and sophisticated form of cybercrime. Their use of Bitcoin as a form of payment allowed them to evade detection and made it difficult for law enforcement agencies to track them down.

Despite their efforts, however, the Bitcoin Bandit was eventually caught and brought to justice. The case serves as a reminder of the importance of taking cybersecurity seriously and taking steps to protect ourselves and our data from the growing threat of ransomware attacks.

The Cemetery Scammer

In 2017, a woman named Brenda Lee Juran was arrested in Pennsylvania for running a cemetery scam. Juran had no affiliation with the cemetery she targeted, but she successfully convinced grieving families that she owned cemetery plots and could sell them at a discounted price.

Juran's scam began to unravel when a family member of one of her victims became suspicious and reported her to the authorities. The investigation that followed revealed that Juran had stolen tens of thousands of dollars from families across Pennsylvania and Ohio.

Juran's scam worked by preying on the vulnerability of grieving families. She would approach families at funerals or through obituaries and offer them discounted plots. Once the families agreed to buy the plots, Juran would demand payment in cash, claiming that the cemetery did not accept credit cards. She would then give the family a fake deed for the plot.

When families later tried to use the plots, they discovered that they did not exist or were already owned by someone else. When they tried to contact Juran to resolve the issue, she would ignore their calls and texts.

Juran was eventually caught when a family member of one of her victims became suspicious and reported her to the authorities. An investigation revealed that Juran had been running the scam for years, stealing tens of thousands of dollars from families across Pennsylvania and Ohio.

Juran was charged with theft by deception, receiving stolen property, and other related offenses. She ultimately pleaded guilty and was sentenced to up to seven years in prison.

The case of the cemetery scammer is a reminder of how vulnerable people can be in times of grief. Scammers often target people when they are at their most vulnerable, and the emotional turmoil of a funeral can make it difficult for families to make clear-headed decisions.

To avoid falling victim to scams like Juran's, it's important to do your due diligence before making any purchases. If someone approaches you with an offer that seems too good to be true, it probably is. Take the time to research the person and the company they claim to represent. Check with the cemetery or funeral home to confirm that the plots are available and that the person selling them has the right to do so.

It's also a good idea to be wary of anyone who demands payment in cash, as this is often a red flag for scams. If you are uncomfortable paying in cash, ask if there are other payment options available.

Finally, if you do fall victim to a scam, don't be afraid to report it to the authorities. Scammers rely on the fact that people are too embarrassed or ashamed to come forward, but reporting the scam can help prevent others from falling victim in the future.

The case of the cemetery scammer is a cautionary tale about the importance of being vigilant and doing your due diligence, especially in times of grief. By taking the time to research offers, being wary of red flags like demands for cash payments, and reporting any suspicious activity to the authorities, we can all help protect ourselves and others from falling victim to scams.

The Baby Extortionist

In 2018, a bizarre and disturbing case of extortion shocked the people of Australia. A woman named Rachel Pfitzner had been leading a double life, faking a pregnancy and then threatening to harm her fake baby unless her ex-partner paid her a large sum of money.

Pfitzner had been involved in a tumultuous relationship with her ex-partner, Blake Davis, and had been trying to conceive a child with him. When she was unable to do so, she decided to fake a pregnancy to keep Davis in her life and extort money from him.

Pfitzner went to great lengths to convince Davis and others that she was pregnant. She gained weight, wore maternity clothes, and even staged a fake baby shower. She also told Davis that she was experiencing complications with the pregnancy and needed money for medical expenses.

As the due date approached, Pfitzner told Davis that she had given birth to a baby boy, whom she named Dylan. She sent him pictures of the baby, which she had taken from the internet, and even pretended to breastfeed him during a video call.

However, Davis became suspicious when Pfitzner refused to let him see the baby in person or take him to a doctor for a check-up. He also discovered that the baby pictures she had been sending him were fake.

Davis confronted Pfitzner about her lies and demanded to see the baby. In response, Pfitzner threatened to harm Dylan unless Davis paid her $4,000. Davis went to the police, and Pfitzner was arrested and charged with extortion.

During her trial, Pfitzner admitted to faking the pregnancy and blackmailing Davis but denied threatening to harm the baby.

However, the court found her guilty of extortion, and she was sentenced to three years and nine months in prison.

The case of the baby extortionist shocked and disgusted many people in Australia, who were appalled by the lengths to which Pfitzner had gone to extort money from her ex-partner. It also raised questions about the psychological factors that could drive someone to engage in such extreme behavior.

Psychologists have noted that some people who engage in extortion may have a personality disorder or be motivated by a desire for power or control. They may also be driven by a sense of entitlement or a belief that they are entitled to compensation for perceived wrongs.

In the case of Rachel Pfitzner, it appears that she may have been motivated by a combination of factors. Her desire for a child, combined with her turbulent relationship with Davis, may have led her to resort to extreme measures to maintain control over him and extort money from him.

The case also highlights the importance of skepticism and caution when it comes to online relationships and communication. Davis was able to uncover Pfitzner's lies and expose her extortion attempts because he questioned her story and sought evidence to confirm her claims.

Overall, the case of the baby extortionist serves as a cautionary tale about the dangers of obsession and the lengths to which some people may go to fulfill their desires. It also highlights the importance of seeking help and support when dealing with difficult and complex personal relationships, rather than resorting to criminal behavior.

The Virtual Lover

In 2019, a man in China was arrested for an unusual case of virtual extortion known as "The Virtual Lover" scam. The man, who remains unnamed, posed as a woman online and tricked a man into sending him money, threatening to release private photos if he did not comply.

The victim, a man from the eastern province of Jiangsu, had reportedly met the suspect online in 2017 and struck up a virtual relationship with him, believing him to be a young woman. The suspect used photos of a young, attractive woman to lure in his victim and gain his trust.

Over the course of two years, the suspect convinced the victim to send him a total of 1.15 million yuan (about $170,000 USD) through online payments and bank transfers. The suspect claimed that the money was for medical expenses, tuition fees, and living expenses, among other things.

However, when the victim started to become suspicious, the suspect threatened to release private photos and information that he had collected over the course of their virtual relationship. The victim was too afraid to go to the police, and continued to send money to the suspect.

It wasn't until late 2019 that the victim finally mustered the courage to report the crime to the police, who launched an investigation into the matter. They were able to trace the suspect to a province in the southwest of China, where he was apprehended and taken into custody.

The case caused a sensation in China, with many people expressing shock and outrage over the suspect's actions. Some commentators pointed out that the case highlights the dangers of online relationships, and the need to be cautious when interacting with strangers on the internet.

The "Virtual Lover" scam is just one example of the many ways that criminals are exploiting the internet and digital technology to commit fraud and extortion. In recent years, there has been a sharp rise in online scams, with criminals using increasingly sophisticated methods to trick people into parting with their money.

One of the most common types of online scams is the "Nigerian prince" scam, where the victim is contacted by someone claiming to be a wealthy foreigner who needs help transferring large sums of money out of their country. The victim is promised a share of the money in exchange for their assistance, but ends up losing money instead.

Another popular scam is the "phishing" scam, where the victim receives an email or message that appears to be from a reputable company or organization, asking them to click on a link and provide personal information. The link leads to a fake website that looks like the real thing, but is actually designed to steal the victim's personal and financial information.

Other examples of online scams include fake online stores, where victims are tricked into buying counterfeit goods or paying for products that never arrive; fake job offers, where victims are asked to pay a fee in exchange for a job that doesn't exist; and fake lottery or prize draw scams, where victims are told they have won a prize but need to pay a fee to claim it.

In order to protect themselves from online scams, experts recommend that people be wary of any unsolicited emails, messages, or phone calls that ask for personal or financial information. They should also be careful about clicking on links in emails or messages, and should always double-check the website's address to ensure that it is legitimate.

The Artful Extortionist

In 2020, a man in Italy was arrested for attempting to extort a large sum of money from the Italian government by threatening to destroy a famous statue located in Florence. The man, later identified as a 41-year-old from Lithuania, had been working as a tour guide in Florence and was apparently familiar with the statue and its value.

The statue in question was a bronze sculpture known as "The Rape of the Sabine Women," created by the Flemish artist Giambologna in the late 16th century. The statue depicts a scene from Roman mythology in which Roman men abduct and marry women from the Sabine tribe. The sculpture is considered one of the most important works of art in Florence and is located in the Loggia dei Lanzi, an open-air museum in the city's historic center.

According to reports, the man had contacted the Italian government and demanded a sum of €100,000 (approximately $118,000) in exchange for not destroying the statue. He threatened to destroy the statue by using a hammer and chisel to remove parts of the bronze sculpture, claiming that he had already made preparations to carry out the act. He allegedly also sent photos of the statue with damage to its head to prove his ability to carry out the threat.

The Italian authorities took the threat seriously and immediately launched an investigation into the matter. They were able to track down the suspect and arrest him before any damage was done to the statue. The man was charged with attempted extortion and damage to a cultural heritage site.

The incident caused concern among art lovers and cultural heritage experts, who expressed their worries about the vulnerability of public art in open-air museums. The incident also raised questions about the security measures in place to protect important works of art.

In response to the incident, the Italian government announced plans to increase security measures around the statue and other works of art in public spaces. The government also stated that it would take legal action to ensure that the man responsible for the threat would be punished to the fullest extent of the law.

The incident involving the artful extortionist is just one example of how valuable works of art can become targets for criminal activity. In recent years, there have been a number of high-profile thefts and attempted thefts of famous works of art, including the theft of several paintings from the Van Gogh Museum in Amsterdam in 1991 and the theft of Edvard Munch's iconic painting "The Scream" from a museum in Oslo in 2004.

While theft and extortion are not new crimes, the use of art as a target for such activity is a relatively recent phenomenon. In the past, criminals would focus on more traditional targets, such as banks or jewelry stores, but as the value of art has increased over the years, so too has the interest of criminals in targeting it.

One reason for this is the fact that art is often considered a "soft" target, meaning that it is often not as well-protected as other valuable items. Many museums and galleries around the world lack the resources or expertise to properly protect their collections, making them vulnerable to theft or damage. In addition, many works of art are easily transportable, making them attractive targets for criminals looking for a quick and easy payout.

The incident in Florence serves as a reminder that the protection of cultural heritage is a shared responsibility. While governments and cultural institutions have a duty to protect their collections, individuals can also play a role in safeguarding works of art by reporting any suspicious activity or behavior.

The Psychic Scammer

In 2021, a woman in California was arrested for a psychic scam that conned people out of large sums of money. The case is a reminder of how people can be easily swindled by those who claim to possess supernatural abilities.

The scammer, Gina Marie Marks, operated under the guise of a psychic medium and convinced her clients that she could communicate with their loved ones who had passed away. She used this pretense to convince her clients that she could help them achieve success, love, and happiness. Marks charged high fees for her services, ranging from a few hundred to several thousand dollars.

Marks' scheme began to unravel when her clients began to suspect that they were being duped. They reported her to the authorities, leading to an investigation. The investigation revealed that Marks had no supernatural abilities and was using simple tricks to convince her clients of her powers. Marks would use common information-gathering techniques, such as cold reading, to gain information about her clients, which she would use to make them believe that she had communicated with their deceased loved ones.

During the investigation, authorities discovered that Marks had scammed more than 20 people, with some victims paying up to $80,000 for her services. Marks was arrested and charged with multiple counts of grand theft and extortion.

The case highlights the danger of trusting individuals who claim to possess psychic abilities. Many scammers use these claims to prey on vulnerable individuals who are seeking answers or guidance. It is essential to be vigilant and cautious when dealing with such individuals and to seek out legitimate sources of help and support.

There are many red flags to watch out for when dealing with psychic scammers. Some of these include the demand for large sums of money upfront, the use of fear tactics or threats to manipulate the victim, and the insistence that they have the power to change the course of events in the victim's life. Genuine psychics will not use these tactics and will instead focus on providing their clients with guidance and support.

It is also important to note that psychic scams are not limited to those who claim to communicate with the dead. Some scammers may claim to possess supernatural abilities such as the ability to read auras or predict the future. Others may use astrology, tarot cards, or other forms of divination to trick their victims.

To avoid falling victim to these types of scams, it is important to approach any psychic or spiritual advisor with a healthy dose of skepticism. Do your research and seek out reviews and testimonials from other clients. Be wary of anyone who promises to deliver quick solutions or guarantees results.

In addition, it is essential to be aware of the legal implications of psychic scams. In many cases, these scams are considered fraud and can result in serious criminal charges. If you have been the victim of a psychic scam, it is important to report the incident to the authorities and seek legal recourse.

The case of the psychic scammer is a stark reminder of the dangers of trusting individuals who claim to possess supernatural abilities. It is essential to be vigilant and cautious when dealing with these types of individuals and to seek out legitimate sources of help and support. By staying informed and aware, we can protect ourselves from these types of scams and avoid falling victim to fraud and deception.

Strange Serial Killers

Albert Fish

Albert Fish, also known as the "Gray Man" and the "Werewolf of Wysteria," was a notorious American serial killer who committed a number of heinous crimes during the early 20th century. Born in 1870 in Washington D.C., Fish had a troubled childhood, with a family history of mental illness and abuse. His father died when he was young, and he was sent to an orphanage where he was frequently beaten and abused. Fish later claimed that he was introduced to sexual activities at a young age by older boys at the orphanage.

As an adult, Fish had a long history of mental illness and was in and out of institutions throughout his life. He married and had six children, but his wife left him for another man, and he was left to raise the children alone. It was during this time that Fish's crimes began.

Fish's first known murder occurred in 1910 when he abducted and killed a young boy in New York. However, he was not caught for this crime until many years later, after his other murders had come to light. Fish's later crimes were particularly brutal, with many of his victims being children. He would often target impoverished families, posing as a harmless old man looking for work or a meal. Once inside the home, he would assault and murder his victims, often mutilating their bodies and even eating their flesh.

Perhaps what is most disturbing about Fish's crimes is the letters he would send to the families of his victims. These letters were often filled with graphic descriptions of his crimes and would sometimes include drawings or photographs. Fish would also taunt the police, often sending letters to newspapers and even to the families of his victims, bragging about his crimes and making bizarre demands.

Despite his disturbing behavior, Fish was able to avoid capture for many years. It was not until 1934 that he was arrested and charged with the murder of 10-year-old Grace Budd. Fish had lured the young girl to his home, where he brutally murdered and dismembered her. After his arrest, Fish made a full confession to this crime and several others, including the murder of the boy in 1910.

Fish's trial was a media sensation, with many newspapers reporting on the disturbing details of his crimes. Despite his confession and the overwhelming evidence against him, Fish pleaded not guilty by reason of insanity. During his trial, Fish claimed that he had been instructed by God to kill and that he had heard voices in his head. However, the jury did not believe his claims of insanity, and he was found guilty and sentenced to death.

Fish was executed in 1936 in the electric chair at Sing Sing prison. His last words reportedly were, "I don't even know why I'm here." His crimes and the graphic details of his letters and confessions have made him one of the most infamous and disturbing serial killers in American history.

Albert Fish was a truly disturbing and brutal serial killer, whose crimes and letters continue to shock and horrify people to this day. Despite his claims of insanity, his crimes demonstrate a high degree of premeditation and sadism. His story serves as a reminder of the dangers of mental illness and the need for greater understanding and treatment for those who suffer from it.

Ted Bundy

Ted Bundy was one of the most notorious serial killers in American history, responsible for the deaths of at least 30 young women in the 1970s. Despite his heinous crimes, Bundy was often described as charming and charismatic, using his good looks and persuasive personality to lure his victims into his grasp.

Bundy was born in Burlington, Vermont, in 1946 and raised by his grandparents. His childhood was marked by instability and abuse, including allegations that his grandfather was physically abusive and his mother suffered from mental illness. Bundy was a bright and ambitious student, however, and went on to attend the University of Washington, where he studied psychology.

It was during his time at university that Bundy began his killing spree, targeting young women in the Seattle area. He was careful to choose victims who resembled his ex-girlfriend, who had broken up with him years earlier, and would often use a fake cast or other disguises to appear less threatening. He would then lure his victims into his car, where he would sexually assault and kill them before disposing of their bodies.

Despite the mounting evidence against him, Bundy managed to evade capture for years, even becoming involved in politics and working on a campaign for a Washington state governor. However, his luck eventually ran out, and he was arrested in 1975 after being pulled over for a routine traffic stop. Police found suspicious items in his car, including handcuffs and other restraints, and Bundy was eventually charged with the murder of a young woman named Caryn Campbell.

Bundy was eventually linked to a string of murders across multiple states, and he was put on trial for the murder of two young women in Florida in 1979. During his trial, Bundy represented himself and managed to charm both the judge and the jury, often appearing confident and in control. However, he was eventually found guilty and sentenced to death.

Despite multiple appeals and attempts to delay his execution, Bundy was finally put to death in 1989 by the electric chair. His execution was watched by crowds of people who had gathered outside the prison, many of whom had lost loved ones to Bundy's brutal crimes.

In the years since his death, Bundy has become something of a cultural phenomenon, with books, movies, and television shows exploring his life and crimes. Many people are fascinated by his apparent charm and charisma, and there is ongoing debate about whether he suffered from mental illness or was simply a calculating and manipulative killer.

Regardless of the reasons behind his crimes, Ted Bundy will always be remembered as one of the most prolific and disturbing serial killers in American history. His ability to charm and manipulate his victims, as well as law enforcement officials and even the public, remains a haunting reminder of the dangers of trusting those who seem too good to be true.

Ed Gein

Ed Gein was an American serial killer and grave robber who was active in the late 1940s and early 1950s. He was born in 1906 in La Crosse County, Wisconsin, and lived with his parents and older brother on a farm in Plainfield, Wisconsin. Gein's father was an alcoholic who was physically abusive towards him and his brother, while his mother was a devoutly religious woman who instilled in him a fear of women and sex.

After his father died in 1940 and his brother passed away in a suspicious fire in 1944, Gein lived alone with his mother on the family farm. When his mother died in 1945, Gein was left alone and began to develop an obsession with death and the human body. He would visit local cemeteries and graveyards to exhume the bodies of recently buried women who he believed resembled his mother. Gein would then take these corpses back to his farm, where he would mutilate them and use their skin and body parts to create various household items, such as lampshades, belts, and masks.

Gein's disturbing behavior came to light in 1957 when he was arrested for the murder of Bernice Worden, a hardware store owner in Plainfield. Worden's son reported her missing, and when police arrived at her store, they discovered that Gein had been the last customer to visit before her disappearance. Upon searching Gein's farm, they found Worden's decapitated body hanging from the rafters, as well as other human remains and various items made from human skin and body parts.

During his interrogation, Gein admitted to the murder of Worden and revealed that he had been involved in the deaths of two other women, Mary Hogan and Evelyn Hartley. Hogan was a tavern owner who was killed in 1954, while Hartley was a 15-year-old girl who disappeared in 1953. Gein claimed to have no memory of the murders, stating that he had gone into a "daze" and did not remember what he had done.

Gein's trial began in 1968, and he was found guilty of the murder of Bernice Worden. Due to his mental state, he was not held responsible for the other murders he had confessed to. Instead, he was sent to a mental institution, where he spent the rest of his life until his death in 1984.

The case of Ed Gein had a significant impact on popular culture, with his story inspiring numerous books, films, and television shows. In particular, Gein served as the inspiration for the character of Norman Bates in the novel and film "Psycho," as well as for the character of Buffalo Bill in the novel and film "The Silence of the Lambs." His fascination with death and the human body has also had an impact on the horror genre, with many works of fiction drawing on themes of body horror and the grotesque.

In addition to his influence on popular culture, Gein's case also had an impact on the field of psychology. Gein's behavior was seen as a manifestation of severe psychological trauma and sexual repression, as well as a possible case of dissociative identity disorder. His obsession with death and the female body was interpreted as a reflection of his own feelings of inadequacy and disgust towards his own sexuality.

The case of Ed Gein remains one of the most disturbing and infamous examples of serial murder in American history. Gein's bizarre and macabre behavior, coupled with his repressed sexuality and severe psychological trauma, has made him a figure of fascination and horror in popular culture. However, it is important to remember that behind the sensationalized accounts of his crimes was a troubled and disturbed individual.

Dennis Rader

Dennis Rader, also known as the "BTK Killer," was a notorious American serial killer who terrorized the community of Wichita, Kansas for 17 years. His nickname stands for "Bind, Torture, Kill," which was his signature method of murdering his victims.

Rader began his killing spree in 1974 when he murdered four members of the Otero family. Over the next several years, he killed a total of ten people, including men, women, and children. He would often stalk his victims for weeks, watching their routines and planning his attacks meticulously.

Rader's murders were characterized by extreme violence and sadism. He would often tie up and torture his victims for hours before finally killing them. He would then pose their bodies in sexually suggestive positions and take pictures of them. He also collected souvenirs from his victims, such as jewelry and clothing.

Despite his gruesome crimes, Rader managed to evade the police for many years. He even taunted them with letters and cryptic messages, which he sent to the media and police. In one letter, he claimed that he was a "monster" and that he couldn't control his urges to kill. In another letter, he included a drawing of a bound woman with a bag over her head.

Throughout the years, Rader continued to commit murders and send letters, which only fueled the police's frustration and desperation to catch him. However, in 2004, Rader made a critical mistake that led to his eventual capture.

He had sent a floppy disk to a local television station in Wichita, which contained metadata that revealed the file had been saved using a computer at the Christ Lutheran Church in Wichita. Investigators traced the computer back to Rader, who was arrested at his home on February 25, 2005.

After his arrest, Rader confessed to all ten murders and was sentenced to ten consecutive life sentences without the possibility of parole. He showed no remorse for his crimes and even joked with the judge during his sentencing hearing. He remains in prison to this day, and his story has been the subject of numerous books, documentaries, and even a feature film.

The case of Dennis Rader is significant not only because of the brutality of his crimes but also because of the way he taunted the police and media. His letters and messages added a layer of psychological terror to the already horrific crimes he committed, making him one of the most infamous serial killers in American history.

In addition, Rader's use of technology to communicate with the media and police was groundbreaking for its time. His floppy disk mistake was one of the first instances in which computer metadata was used to identify a suspect, leading to a significant breakthrough in forensic technology.

The case of Dennis Rader is a chilling reminder of the horrors that can be perpetrated by those who seem the least likely to do harm. His outward appearance as a loving husband, father, and church leader concealed a dark and twisted side that led to the deaths of ten innocent people. The fact that he was able to evade capture for so many years and continue to torment his victims' families through his letters and messages only adds to the horror of his crimes.

Jeffrey Dahmer

Jeffrey Dahmer, also known as the Milwaukee Cannibal, was an American serial killer and sex offender who committed the murders of 17 men and boys between 1978 and 1991. Dahmer is known for his gruesome crimes, including cannibalism, necrophilia, and preservation of body parts.

Born on May 21, 1960, in Milwaukee, Wisconsin, Dahmer had a difficult childhood. He was an introverted child who had few friends and struggled with social skills. He also suffered from several medical conditions, including a double hernia and a speech impediment, which made him the target of bullies at school.

As a teenager, Dahmer's behavior became increasingly erratic. He began to drink heavily and often got into trouble with the law. In 1978, he was arrested for indecent exposure and later that year, he was charged with drugging and molesting a 13-year-old boy. Despite his criminal behavior, Dahmer was able to graduate from high school and attend Ohio State University for one semester before dropping out.

Dahmer's killing spree began in 1978 when he picked up a hitchhiker, took him back to his parents' home, and killed him. Over the next 13 years, Dahmer killed a total of 17 men and boys, most of whom were of Asian or African American descent.

Dahmer's methods of killing varied, but he often used drugs to sedate his victims before strangling them to death. He then dismembered their bodies and engaged in necrophilia and cannibalism. Dahmer also tried to create "zombies" by injecting acid into his victims' brains in an attempt to create a submissive, living sex partner.

Despite his horrific crimes, Dahmer was able to evade detection for many years. He was finally caught in 1991 when one of his intended victims escaped and flagged down police. When police searched

Dahmer's apartment, they found evidence of his crimes, including preserved body parts and photographs of his victims.

During his trial, Dahmer pleaded guilty but insane. He claimed that he had a compulsion to kill and that he had been driven to commit his crimes due to feelings of loneliness and rejection. However, the jury found Dahmer guilty of 15 counts of murder and he was sentenced to 15 consecutive life sentences.

While in prison, Dahmer expressed remorse for his crimes and underwent therapy. He also converted to Christianity and was baptized by a local pastor. However, his attempts at rehabilitation were cut short when he was beaten to death by a fellow inmate in 1994.

Dahmer's crimes shocked the nation and sparked a debate about the death penalty and mental illness. Some argued that Dahmer should have been executed for his crimes, while others pointed to his history of mental illness and argued that he should receive treatment instead.

Dahmer's case also raised questions about the role of law enforcement in investigating missing persons cases, particularly in cases involving marginalized communities. Many of Dahmer's victims were young men of color, and their disappearances were not taken seriously by law enforcement.

Today, Jeffrey Dahmer is remembered as one of the most notorious serial killers in American history. His crimes continue to fascinate and horrify people, and his story has been the subject of numerous books, documentaries, and films. Despite the passage of time, the memory of Dahmer's victims lives on, and their families continue to mourn their loss.

Andrei Chikatilo

Andrei Chikatilo, also known as the "Butcher of Rostov," was a Ukrainian-born Russian serial killer who murdered at least 52 people, mostly young boys and girls, between 1978 and 1990. He was born in 1936 in the small village of Yabluchne in the Ukrainian SSR, now Ukraine, and grew up in a troubled family during the Stalinist era.

Chikatilo had a difficult childhood, being born during the Holodomor famine that killed millions of people in Ukraine, and his father was taken away by Stalin's secret police when he was a child. His mother was abusive and overprotective, and Chikatilo had problems with bedwetting, leading to bullying and humiliation by his peers. He was a shy and introverted child who struggled in school and had few friends.

Chikatilo served in the Soviet Army and then worked as a teacher before being fired for his inappropriate behavior with children. He then worked as a factory worker and a supply clerk, all the while struggling with his sexual impulses towards children and his inability to have normal relationships with adults. He married in 1963 and had two children, but his sexual problems persisted, and he began to have violent fantasies about young girls.

In 1978, Chikatilo committed his first murder, that of a nine-year-old girl. He lured her into a forest near Shakhty, a town in the Rostov Oblast of Russia, where he stabbed her to death and mutilated her body. He then went on to commit a series of similar murders over the next 12 years, mostly in the same region of Russia, targeting young boys and girls who were runaways or from troubled families.

Chikatilo's modus operandi was to lure his victims to remote locations, usually under the pretense of offering them a job or some other opportunity, and then attack them with a knife. He would often mutilate their genitals and other body parts, sometimes eating them or taking them as souvenirs. He was known to be extremely sadistic and would often prolong his victims' suffering by torturing them before killing them.

Despite the high number of victims and the gruesome nature of the murders, Chikatilo managed to evade capture for many years. He was finally arrested in 1990 when a witness saw him with a young girl and reported him to the police. He was found with a knife and other suspicious items, and his DNA was later matched to semen samples found on some of the victims' bodies.

Chikatilo was convicted of 52 murders and sentenced to death in 1992. During his trial, he showed no remorse for his crimes and even taunted the families of his victims. He claimed that he was driven to kill by his uncontrollable sexual urges and that he hoped his execution would put an end to his suffering.

Chikatilo's case was notable for its brutality and the length of time he was able to evade capture. It also highlighted the Soviet Union's problems with mental illness and the lack of resources for treating people with sexual disorders or other psychological problems. His case has been the subject of numerous books, movies, and TV shows, and he is often cited as one of the most infamous serial killers in history.

In conclusion, Andrei Chikatilo was a Ukrainian-born Russian serial killer who murdered at least 52 people, mostly young boys and girls, over a period of 12 years. He was known as the "Butcher of Rostov" and was infamous for the brutal and sadistic nature of his crimes. His case highlighted the problems of mental illness and sexual disorders in the Soviet Union, as well as the challenges of tracking and capturing serial killers.

John Wayne Gacy

John Wayne Gacy was an American serial killer who committed the murders of 33 young men and boys between 1972 and 1978. He was also known as the "Killer Clown" due to his work as a children's party entertainer and his penchant for dressing up as a clown.

Gacy was born in Chicago, Illinois in 1942. He was the only son of three children and had a troubled relationship with his father, who was physically abusive towards him. Gacy was also overweight and suffered from health problems, which made him a target for bullying at school.

Despite his difficulties, Gacy managed to graduate from high school and went on to attend business college. He married his high school sweetheart, Marlynn Myers, in 1964 and had two children with her. The family moved to Iowa in 1966, where Gacy started his own construction business.

Gacy's life took a dark turn in the early 1970s when he was arrested for sexually assaulting a teenage boy. He was sentenced to ten years in prison but was released after serving only 18 months. He then moved back to Chicago and resumed his construction business.

It was during this time that Gacy began his killing spree. He targeted young men and boys, many of whom were runaways or hustlers. He would lure them to his home with the promise of work or money, then drug and sexually assault them before strangling them to death. He buried most of their bodies in the crawlspace beneath his home, while others were disposed of in nearby rivers.

Gacy's crimes went undetected for several years, despite his frequent interactions with police and his known history of sexual assault. It wasn't until 1978 that he was finally caught, thanks in part to the persistence of a young man named Robert Piest.

Piest had gone missing after telling his mother that he was going to meet with Gacy about a job. When police questioned Gacy, he denied any knowledge of Piest's whereabouts. However, they later obtained a search warrant for his home and uncovered evidence of his crimes, including human bones and teeth.

Gacy was arrested and charged with multiple counts of murder. He initially attempted to plead insanity, claiming that he had multiple personalities, but this defense was ultimately rejected by the court. In 1980, he was found guilty of all charges and sentenced to death.

During his time on death row, Gacy became an infamous figure in the media. He granted interviews to journalists and even painted a series of disturbing portraits depicting clowns and other eerie figures. He was executed by lethal injection in 1994, bringing an end to one of the most notorious killing sprees in American history.

The case of John Wayne Gacy continues to fascinate and horrify people to this day. His use of a clown persona and his seemingly normal exterior have made him a symbol of the dangers of hidden evil lurking in society. His crimes have been the subject of numerous books, films, and TV shows, and his legacy as a monstrous figure of American crime is firmly cemented in history.

Richard Ramirez

Richard Ramirez, also known as the "Night Stalker," was a notorious American serial killer who terrorized Southern California in the mid-1980s. Born on February 29, 1960, in El Paso, Texas, Ramirez was one of five children in a large, working-class Mexican-American family. Ramirez's childhood was marred by poverty and abuse. His father was a former police officer who physically abused his wife and children, and Ramirez was often left alone in the family's apartment with his younger siblings while his parents worked.

As a teenager, Ramirez became interested in Satanism and started using drugs. He dropped out of high school and began living a life of crime, committing burglaries and stealing cars. In 1982, he moved to California and started his killing spree, which lasted for over a year and a half.

Ramirez's modus operandi was to break into homes in the middle of the night and attack his victims while they were asleep. He would use a variety of weapons, including knives, hammers, and guns, to kill and maim his victims. His victims were chosen at random and included men, women, and children.

During his spree, Ramirez killed 13 people and injured several others. He often left Satanic symbols and messages at the crime scenes, which added to the fear and confusion surrounding the case. The media dubbed him the "Night Stalker," and his face became ubiquitous on television and in newspapers.

Despite the intense media coverage, Ramirez managed to evade police for several months. He was finally captured in August 1985, after a group of citizens in East Los Angeles recognized him from a police sketch and tackled him to the ground.

Ramirez's trial was one of the most sensational in California's history. He was charged with 13 counts of murder, five counts of attempted murder, 11 counts of sexual assault, and 14 counts of burglary. Ramirez showed no remorse for his crimes and often smiled and waved at the cameras during his court appearances.

In 1989, Ramirez was convicted on all charges and sentenced to death. While on death row, he continued to receive attention from the media and was often interviewed by reporters. Ramirez died on June 7, 2013, in a hospital in Greenbrae, California, while awaiting execution.

Ramirez's crimes shocked and terrified Southern California, and his case became a symbol of the danger of random violence. His use of Satanic symbols and the media's coverage of his case also contributed to the rise of Satanic panic in the United States in the 1980s.

Ramirez's case is also notable for the controversial role played by forensic science. The prosecution relied heavily on forensic evidence, including shoe prints and DNA samples, to link Ramirez to the crimes. However, the defense argued that the evidence was contaminated and unreliable, and that the police had coerced a false confession out of Ramirez.

Despite these controversies, Ramirez's legacy as a brutal and sadistic killer is well established. His case continues to fascinate and horrify true crime enthusiasts and the general public alike.

Aileen Wuornos

Aileen Wuornos was born on February 29, 1956, in Rochester, Michigan. Her parents were both teenagers when she was born, and her father was a convicted child molester who hanged himself in prison when Wuornos was only 13 years old. Her mother abandoned her and her brother, leaving them to live with their abusive grandparents.

Wuornos became sexually active at a young age and was pregnant by the time she was 14. She gave birth to a boy, whom she put up for adoption. She was kicked out of her grandparents' house and left to fend for herself. She turned to prostitution to survive and began hitchhiking around the country.

In 1989, Wuornos was working as a prostitute in Florida when she met Tyria Moore, a woman who became her lover and partner in crime. Wuornos claimed that she killed seven men in self-defense, all of whom had tried to rape or assault her while she was working as a prostitute.

Her first victim was Richard Mallory, a convicted rapist who picked her up for sex. Wuornos claimed that he had tried to rape her, and she shot him in self-defense. Her next victim was David Spears, whom she said had threatened her with a gun. She also killed Charles Carskaddon, Peter Siems, Troy Burress, Charles Humphreys, and Walter Antonio.

Wuornos and Moore were eventually caught when they were found driving one of their victims' cars. Wuornos confessed to the murders and was convicted of seven counts of first-degree murder. She was sentenced to death and executed by lethal injection on October 9, 2002.

Wuornos' case became famous due to her claims of self-defense and the fact that she was a female serial killer, which was relatively rare at the time. Her life has been the subject of books, documentaries, and movies, including the 2003 film "Monster," for which Charlize Theron won an Academy Award for her portrayal of Wuornos.

However, some have criticized the media's portrayal of Wuornos, arguing that she was not a sympathetic figure and that her claims of self-defense may not have been entirely truthful. Some have also pointed out that Wuornos had a history of violence and had been in trouble with the law before her killing spree, including an incident in which she hit a man with a beer bottle and a robbery that landed her in jail for several years.

Despite the controversy surrounding her case, Wuornos remains a fascinating figure in the world of true crime. Her story sheds light on the lives of those who live on the margins of society, as well as the often-complex psychology of serial killers.

Gary Ridgway

Gary Ridgway, also known as the "Green River Killer," is one of the most notorious American serial killers, responsible for the murders of at least 49 women in the Seattle area during the 1980s and 1990s.

Ridgway was born on February 18, 1949, in Salt Lake City, Utah. He was the middle child of three brothers and grew up in a dysfunctional family. Ridgway had a troubled childhood, as his parents frequently argued and his mother was known to be domineering and emotionally abusive towards her sons.

As a teenager, Ridgway began to exhibit disturbing behavior, including necrophilia and a fascination with dead animals. He also had difficulty forming relationships with women and was unable to maintain a stable romantic relationship.

In 1982, the bodies of several young women began turning up in the Green River area of King County, Washington. The killer was dubbed the "Green River Killer" by the media. The victims were mostly young women who were working as prostitutes or runaway teenagers.

For years, police were unable to catch the killer, and the number of victims continued to rise. In 1984, Ridgway was questioned by police and asked to take a polygraph test. He passed the test and was not considered a suspect at the time.

However, the investigation into the Green River Killer continued, and in 2001, Ridgway was arrested and charged with the murders of four women. He later pleaded guilty to a total of 49 murders in exchange for avoiding the death penalty.

Ridgway's modus operandi was to pick up prostitutes or runaways and take them to secluded areas where he would strangle them to death. He would then dump their bodies in the Green River or other remote locations. Ridgway often returned to the dump sites to have sex with the bodies, and he kept many of the victims' personal belongings as trophies.

Ridgway's arrest and confession shocked the nation, as he had been married for many years and had worked as a truck painter. He was a quiet and unassuming man who did not fit the typical profile of a serial killer.

During his trial, Ridgway was described as a cold, emotionless killer who showed no remorse for his crimes. He was sentenced to life in prison without the possibility of parole.

Despite his guilty plea and confession to 49 murders, some investigators believe that Ridgway may have killed many more women. He was known to have had a high sex drive and would often engage in sex with prostitutes, suggesting that there may have been many more victims who were never identified.

Ridgway's case is notable for the length of time it took to catch him, as well as the number of victims he claimed. His capture was due in part to advances in DNA technology, which allowed investigators to match DNA evidence found at the crime scenes to Ridgway's DNA.

The Green River Killer's reign of terror left a lasting impact on the Seattle area, as well as the families of the victims. Many of the victims were young women who were vulnerable and marginalized, and their deaths were often ignored or overlooked by law enforcement.

In the years since his conviction, Ridgway has remained in prison, occasionally making headlines for his behavior behind bars. He has been attacked by fellow inmates, and in 2006, he was caught with a smuggled cell phone in his cell.

Peculiar Ponzi Schemes

Charles Ponzi

Charles Ponzi was an Italian businessman who became infamous for orchestrating one of the most notorious financial frauds in history, now known as the Ponzi scheme. Born in Lugo, Italy, in 1882, Ponzi was a charismatic individual who had a talent for making people believe in him. He immigrated to the United States in 1903 and worked odd jobs before becoming a con man.

The Ponzi scheme that made Charles Ponzi a household name began in 1919 when he founded the Securities Exchange Company in Boston. He promised investors returns of up to 50% in just 90 days by taking advantage of differences in international postal reply coupons. The coupons were sold at a discounted price in some countries and could be redeemed for full postage in other countries. Ponzi claimed he could buy the coupons in one country, exchange them for more valuable stamps in another country, and then sell the stamps at a profit in the US.

The scheme was simple but alluring, and it caught on quickly. People were drawn to Ponzi's promise of easy and quick profits. In fact, they were so eager to invest that Ponzi made $5,000 in his first three hours of business. By the end of the first month, he had made $420,000.

However, there was a fundamental flaw in Ponzi's plan. The number of coupons needed to make a profit was vastly greater than the number of coupons available in circulation. In other words, Ponzi was taking money from new investors to pay off earlier investors. He was not making a profit through legitimate business means.

To keep up the charade, Ponzi began paying off his early investors using funds from newer ones. Word of the scheme began to spread, and Ponzi's company grew larger and larger. He even started offering free tours of his office to show investors how he was making so much money.

As the scheme grew, Ponzi's personal wealth also grew. He bought expensive cars, expensive clothes, and even a mansion. He was living the high life, but it was all based on lies and deceit.

By July 1920, the Securities Exchange Company was making $250,000 a day, but the scheme was starting to unravel. Reporters began investigating and exposing Ponzi's fraudulent activities. The US Post Office began to investigate, and eventually, the Securities Exchange Company was shut down.

In August 1920, Ponzi was arrested and charged with 86 counts of mail fraud. He was found guilty and sentenced to five years in prison. However, he was released after only three and a half years for good behavior. He was later convicted of a similar crime in Florida and served an additional seven years.

The Ponzi scheme that Charles Ponzi invented has become synonymous with financial fraud. The scheme has been replicated numerous times, often with slight variations, by others seeking to make quick money. The basic concept of the Ponzi scheme remains the same: investors are promised high returns in a short amount of time, but the returns are not generated through legitimate business means.

The Charles Ponzi's scheme was a classic example of how the promise of easy money can cloud people's judgment. Ponzi was a master of deception, using his charisma to lure investors into a fraudulent scheme that promised high returns with little risk. He took advantage of people's greed and desperation, leaving many ruined in his wake. Although Ponzi died in 1949, his legacy lives on in the form of copycat schemes that continue to defraud people to this day.

The Airplane Scheme

In 2014, a man named David Joseph Prentice from Florida was found to have run a Ponzi scheme centered around buying and reselling airplanes. Prentice promised investors returns of up to 35%, claiming that he had a team of aviation experts and financiers who would help him purchase planes at discounted rates, fix them up, and sell them for a profit. However, the whole operation was a fraud, and Prentice was using the money he raised to fund his extravagant lifestyle and pay off earlier investors.

The scheme began to unravel in 2013 when some investors started to become suspicious and demanded to see the aircraft they had supposedly invested in. Prentice was unable to provide any evidence that the planes existed or that he had made any sales. He told his investors that the deals had fallen through due to issues with financing and regulatory approvals, but promised to make things right by finding new buyers and closing the deals.

In reality, Prentice had never purchased any airplanes and had no intention of doing so. Instead, he had used the money he raised to pay for personal expenses, including luxury cars, private jets, and a $10,000 a month rental home. He also used the money to pay off earlier investors, using their funds to create the appearance of profits and to prevent them from sounding the alarm to authorities.

By the time the scheme was uncovered, Prentice had defrauded dozens of investors out of millions of dollars. He was arrested and charged with multiple counts of fraud and money laundering. In 2016, he was sentenced to 12 years in prison and ordered to pay more than $8 million in restitution to his victims.

The Airplane Scheme was an example of a classic Ponzi scheme, in which early investors are paid with funds raised from later investors rather than from legitimate profits. Prentice promised his investors high returns in a short amount of time, using the lure of aviation investment as a way to attract people who may have been looking for a way to diversify their portfolios or earn quick money. By preying on their greed and desperation, Prentice was able to raise millions of dollars without ever having to deliver on his promises.

One of the most alarming aspects of this scheme is the fact that Prentice was able to convince so many people to invest in an industry that they knew little about. Aviation investment is a complex and highly regulated field, requiring a great deal of expertise and experience to navigate successfully. Prentice had no background in aviation and no evidence of a team of experts, yet was able to convince investors that he had the knowledge and connections necessary to make money in the industry.

Another notable aspect of The Airplane Scheme is the way in which Prentice used the money he raised to fund his own lavish lifestyle. Like many Ponzi schemers, he was more interested in lining his own pockets than in actually making legitimate investments. He spent millions of dollars on luxury goods and services, creating a facade of success that he used to attract even more investors.

The Airplane Scheme is a cautionary tale for anyone considering investing in a high-risk, high-reward opportunity. It is important to do your due diligence and research any investment opportunity thoroughly before handing over your hard-earned money. While it may be tempting to believe in the promises of high returns and easy money, the reality is that there are few legitimate investments that can deliver such results.

The Rubber Ball Scheme

In the 1920s, a man named Leo Koretz, also known as the "Midwest Ponzi," devised a peculiar Ponzi scheme that promised investors returns of up to 200% on their investments in the rubber ball industry. The scheme became known as the "Rubber Ball Scheme," and it resulted in the loss of millions of dollars.

Koretz, a lawyer and businessman from Chicago, convinced people to invest in his scheme by claiming that he had discovered a new process for making rubber balls. He promised investors that he would buy rubber from plantations in Brazil, transport it to his factory in Chicago, and then manufacture and sell rubber balls at a significant profit. Koretz claimed that he had already secured contracts with major retailers, including Sears Roebuck and Co. and Montgomery Ward, to sell his rubber balls.

Investors were lured in by Koretz's charming personality and the promise of high returns. Many invested their life savings, and some even mortgaged their homes to invest in the scheme. Koretz used the money to maintain an extravagant lifestyle, including purchasing a luxury home, a yacht, and a private plane.

However, there was no new process for making rubber balls, and Koretz had no contracts with major retailers. Instead, he used the money from new investors to pay off earlier investors and cover his own debts. To maintain the illusion of success, Koretz sent investors false reports on the progress of his company, complete with fake photographs of rubber ball factories and plantations in Brazil.

The scheme began to unravel in 1923 when a few investors started to ask questions about the lack of profits. Koretz tried to calm their fears by showing them his factory and other assets, but he couldn't provide any evidence of the contracts with major retailers.

Eventually, the scheme collapsed, and investors lost an estimated $20 million, which would be over $300 million in today's currency.

Koretz fled to Canada and then Europe, but he was eventually captured and brought back to the United States to face charges. He was found guilty of mail fraud and sentenced to 10 years in prison. While in prison, he wrote a memoir titled "The Collapse of a Crooked Lawyer," which detailed his life and the scheme.

The Rubber Ball Scheme is a classic example of a Ponzi scheme, named after Charles Ponzi, who conducted a similar scheme in the early 1900s. Ponzi schemes are named after Charles Ponzi, an Italian immigrant who became famous for his fraudulent investment scheme in the early 20th century. Ponzi promised investors a 50% return on their investment in just 45 days by buying and selling international postal reply coupons. However, he was actually using the money from new investors to pay off earlier investors, and the scheme eventually collapsed, causing investors to lose millions of dollars.

Ponzi schemes work by enticing investors with promises of high returns in a short amount of time. The scheme is able to continue as long as there are enough new investors to pay off earlier investors. However, the scheme eventually collapses when there are not enough new investors to cover the payouts, and investors lose their money.

The Rubber Ball Scheme is a cautionary tale about the dangers of investing in something that seems too good to be true. Koretz's promises of high returns on investments in the rubber ball industry were nothing more than a ploy to take investors' money and enrich himself. The scheme resulted in the loss of millions of dollars and ruined the lives of many investors. It is a reminder to always do your due diligence before investing your money and to be wary of promises of high returns in a short amount of time.

The Cemetery Scheme

The world of financial fraud is riddled with countless scams that have bilked unsuspecting investors out of billions of dollars. One such scheme that came to light in 2009 was the Cemetery Scheme, which involved a Texas man using his company to defraud investors by promising them high returns on their investments in the cemetery industry. While the scam may have seemed unusual, it followed a classic pattern of Ponzi schemes, with the perpetrator using new investors' money to pay off earlier investors and enrich himself.

The man behind the Cemetery Scheme was named Theodore (Ted) L. Nelson, who owned and operated a company called Forever After. According to the company's marketing material, Forever After claimed to provide investors with the opportunity to invest in the rapidly growing cemetery industry, which the company claimed was worth $25 billion annually in the United States alone. The company offered investors the opportunity to purchase "burial plots" in advance, which they could then resell at a profit in the future as the demand for cemetery space increased.

To lure in potential investors, Nelson promised returns of up to 12%, which he claimed were generated by purchasing and reselling cemetery plots at a profit. Nelson convinced investors that their money would be used to buy land in strategic locations, where cemeteries were in high demand. However, in reality, he used the investors' money to fund his lavish lifestyle, which included buying a $3 million home, a $1 million yacht, and an $80,000 Hummer.

As with many Ponzi schemes, the scam began to unravel when Nelson was no longer able to pay the returns he promised to investors. Instead of acknowledging the problem, Nelson attempted to cover up his wrongdoing by using new investors' money to pay off earlier investors. To make the scam appear legitimate, Nelson even went to the extent of creating fake documents, such as deeds and other legal paperwork, to make it seem as if the investments were real.

However, when the economy began to take a turn for the worse, it became increasingly difficult for Nelson to attract new investors. As a result, he was no longer able to pay the returns he promised to earlier investors. Eventually, the scheme collapsed, and investors began to demand their money back. When they were unable to get their money, they contacted the authorities.

In 2009, Nelson was arrested and charged with 11 counts of wire fraud, three counts of mail fraud, and three counts of money laundering. He was also charged with engaging in organized criminal activity, which carried a maximum sentence of life in prison. Nelson initially pleaded not guilty to the charges but later changed his plea to guilty.

At his sentencing hearing, Nelson's victims testified about how they had lost their life savings, their homes, and their retirement funds due to the scam. One victim spoke about how he had been promised returns of up to 12%, which he believed were generated from the sale of cemetery plots. He said that he had invested his entire retirement savings of $200,000 with Nelson, but had received no returns and had lost everything.

In 2011, Nelson was sentenced to 25 years in prison and ordered to pay restitution of $120 million to his victims. In addition, the court ordered the forfeiture of Nelson's assets, including his home, yacht, and Hummer. Despite his conviction, many of Nelson's victims were left with nothing, and the scam served as a stark reminder of the dangers of investing in schemes that promise high returns with little risk.

The Coconut Plantation Scheme

In the 1970s, the promise of a quick profit drew many people to invest in a coconut plantation on the island of Kauai in Hawaii. The man behind the scheme, Ronald Rewald, claimed to be a Harvard-educated investment guru and convinced many people to part with their savings.

Rewald set up a company called Bishop, Baldwin, Rewald, Dillingham, and Wong (BBRDW) to sell land in the supposed coconut plantation. He promised investors a return of up to 250% on their investment, claiming that the land was highly valuable and would yield high profits.

The scheme seemed to work at first, and Rewald became wealthy by selling land to eager investors. He spent his money on a lavish lifestyle, including a private jet, expensive cars, and luxury vacations.

However, the truth was that there was no coconut plantation. The land that Rewald sold to investors was worthless, and he was simply using their money to fund his own lifestyle. He also used the money to pay off earlier investors, as the scheme depended on a constant flow of new investors to keep it going.

The scheme started to unravel when investors began to demand their returns. Rewald was unable to pay them, and in 1983, the Securities and Exchange Commission (SEC) started an investigation into BBRDW.

During the investigation, it was discovered that Rewald had been forging documents and lying about his credentials. He had never attended Harvard and had no real investment experience. In fact, he had a criminal record for embezzlement and had previously served time in prison.

Rewald was eventually arrested and charged with securities fraud. He was found guilty and sentenced to 20 years in prison. The investors who had lost their money in the scheme were never fully compensated, as most of the money had been spent by Rewald.

The Coconut Plantation Scheme is a classic example of a Ponzi scheme, where investors are promised high returns but are actually paid from the money of later investors rather than from actual profits. In this case, the supposed profits came from the sale of land that did not exist.

The scheme also highlights the importance of due diligence when investing. Many of the investors in the Coconut Plantation Scheme were taken in by Rewald's claims of being a Harvard-educated investment guru, without bothering to verify his credentials or investigate the supposed coconut plantation.

Furthermore, the scheme also highlights the dangers of greed. The promise of quick profits can blind investors to the risks involved and lead them to make unwise decisions. In the case of the Coconut Plantation Scheme, many investors lost their life savings due to their eagerness to make a quick profit.

In the end, the Coconut Plantation Scheme left many people with nothing but empty promises and financial ruin. While Ronald Rewald may have enjoyed a lavish lifestyle for a time, his greed ultimately led to his downfall and imprisonment.

The Beanie Baby Scheme

In the 1990s, Beanie Babies became a craze in the United States. These small stuffed animals, filled with plastic pellets, were sold by Ty Inc. and marketed as collectibles. The popularity of Beanie Babies led to a boom in the secondary market, where people bought and sold them for profit. It also led to the creation of a Ponzi scheme centered around Beanie Babies.

In 1996, a woman named Peggy Jo Hooper started a company called Peggy Jo Hooper Enterprises, which she used to sell Beanie Babies. She began offering investment opportunities to her customers, promising high returns on their investment by buying and reselling Beanie Babies. She claimed that she had connections with Ty Inc. that allowed her to purchase large quantities of Beanie Babies at a discounted price.

As more people invested in her company, Hooper expanded her operations. She opened a store in Las Vegas, started a catalog business, and even appeared on television shows like QVC to promote her investment opportunities. She claimed that her investments were safe and that she had a track record of success.

However, Hooper's investments were not safe. She was not buying and selling Beanie Babies as she claimed. Instead, she was using the money she received from new investors to pay off earlier investors. She was also using the money to fund her own lavish lifestyle, which included expensive cars, jewelry, and vacations.

Hooper's scheme came crashing down in 1999 when the Securities and Exchange Commission (SEC) began investigating her company. They found that she had raised over $30 million from investors and had used the majority of it for personal expenses. In 2000, Hooper was indicted on charges of fraud, money laundering, and tax evasion.

During her trial, Hooper claimed that she had not intended to defraud her investors and that she had believed her investments were legitimate. However, the jury did not believe her and found her guilty on all counts. She was sentenced to 10 years in prison and was ordered to pay restitution to her victims.

The Beanie Baby Ponzi scheme was one of the most bizarre schemes of the 1990s. It took advantage of the craze surrounding Beanie Babies and the willingness of people to invest in anything that promised high returns. However, it also showed the dangers of blindly investing in something without doing proper research.

The aftermath of the Beanie Baby scheme had lasting effects on the Beanie Baby market. As news of the scheme broke, the secondary market for Beanie Babies began to collapse. Prices plummeted, and many people lost money on their investments. The scheme also damaged the reputation of Ty Inc., which had nothing to do with Hooper's fraudulent activities.

The Beanie Baby Ponzi scheme was a cautionary tale about the dangers of greed and the willingness of people to invest in anything that promised high returns. Peggy Jo Hooper used the popularity of Beanie Babies to lure investors into a scheme that promised them wealth but ultimately left them with nothing. The scheme also had lasting effects on the Beanie Baby market, showing the importance of doing proper research before investing in anything.

The Water Filtration Scheme

The Water Filtration Scheme was a Ponzi scheme that was operated by an Indiana man named Timothy McQueen. McQueen promised investors returns of up to 44% by selling them water filtration systems. However, he was actually using the money to fund his own lifestyle and pay off earlier investors.

McQueen began his scheme in 2015 and quickly attracted a number of investors. He told them that he had developed a new type of water filtration system that was superior to anything on the market. He claimed that the system could remove impurities from water that other filters could not.

McQueen sold his filters to both residential and commercial customers. He convinced investors that the demand for his product was so high that he needed to expand his business. He promised them that he would use their money to purchase more equipment and hire more staff.

However, McQueen never actually produced any new filters. Instead, he used the money he received from new investors to pay off earlier investors. He also used the funds to support his own lifestyle, which included luxury cars and expensive vacations.

As more investors got involved, McQueen had to continue to recruit new ones in order to keep the scheme going. He used a variety of tactics to convince people to invest, including attending trade shows and seminars and giving presentations on the benefits of his filtration system.

Despite the fact that McQueen was not producing any new filters, he continued to convince investors that his business was growing. He provided them with fake financial statements that showed a high rate of return on their investment. He also sent out regular newsletters that described the supposed successes of his business.

However, McQueen's scheme began to unravel in 2017 when some investors became suspicious and began to investigate. They discovered that he had never actually produced any new filters and that he was using the money to pay off earlier investors.

In October of that year, McQueen was arrested and charged with securities fraud. He eventually pled guilty and was sentenced to 10 years in prison.

The Water Filtration Scheme was a classic example of a Ponzi scheme. McQueen promised investors high returns on their investment, but he was not actually using the money to produce any new products or services. Instead, he was using the money to pay off earlier investors and support his own lifestyle.

Investors should always be wary of investment opportunities that promise high returns with little or no risk. They should also be skeptical of investment opportunities that are not backed up by concrete evidence of a successful business model.

In the case of the Water Filtration Scheme, investors were drawn in by McQueen's promises of high returns and the supposed success of his business. However, they should have been more skeptical of his claims and asked for proof of his success.

The Water Filtration Scheme also demonstrates the importance of due diligence. Investors should always investigate the background of the person or company offering an investment opportunity. They should also investigate the underlying business model and make sure that it is viable.

The Water Filtration Scheme was a Ponzi scheme that promised investors high returns on their investment but was not actually using the money to produce any new products or services. The scheme ultimately collapsed when investors became suspicious and discovered the truth.

The Olive Oil Scheme

The Olive Oil Scheme was a fraudulent investment operation that promised investors high returns through the buying and reselling of high-end olive oil. It was led by a man named Scott Cameron in California in 2010. Cameron promised investors returns of up to 140% on their investments, claiming that he had connections in the olive oil industry that would allow him to purchase the oil at a discount and sell it at a significant markup.

Cameron's pitch was enticing, and he quickly attracted a group of investors who were eager to get in on the lucrative opportunity. He promised them that their investments were safe and that they would receive a return on their investment within just a few months. Cameron was a charismatic salesman, and many of his investors trusted him implicitly.

However, the Olive Oil Scheme was nothing more than a Ponzi scheme. Cameron was using the money from new investors to pay off earlier investors and fund his own lavish lifestyle. He had no connections in the olive oil industry, and he was not actually buying or selling any olive oil.

As more and more investors poured their money into the scheme, Cameron's debts began to mount. He was unable to keep up with the promised returns, and he began to stall his investors by making excuses for why they weren't receiving their payments. Eventually, the scheme collapsed, and Cameron disappeared with the investors' money.

The fallout from the Olive Oil Scheme was significant. Many investors lost their life savings, and some were forced to declare bankruptcy. Cameron was eventually caught and sentenced to 10 years in prison for his role in the scheme.

The Olive Oil Scheme is just one example of the many Ponzi schemes that have been perpetrated over the years. These schemes are named after Charles Ponzi, who ran a similar scheme in the early 20th century. In a Ponzi scheme, the operator promises high returns to investors, but instead of using the money to invest in legitimate businesses, they use it to pay off earlier investors and fund their own lifestyle.

Ponzi schemes can be devastating for investors, as they often lose all of their money when the scheme collapses. They can also have wider economic impacts, as the collapse of a large Ponzi scheme can cause significant financial instability.

To avoid falling victim to a Ponzi scheme, it is important to be wary of any investment opportunity that promises high returns with little risk. Investors should do their due diligence and research the company and its management before investing any money. They should also be skeptical of any investment opportunity that is pitched by a charismatic salesperson, as this can be a red flag for a potential Ponzi scheme.

The Olive Oil Scheme was a fraudulent investment operation that promised investors high returns through the buying and reselling of high-end olive oil. It was led by a man named Scott Cameron in California in 2010, and it collapsed when Cameron was unable to keep up with the promised returns. The scheme is just one example of the many Ponzi schemes that have been perpetrated over the years, and investors should be wary of any investment opportunity that promises high returns with little risk.

The Debt Elimination Scheme

In the early 2000s, Brent Austin of Florida introduced a debt elimination program called "The Miracle Money Method" that promised investors high returns of up to 10 times their investment by using a secret method to eliminate their debts. Unfortunately, the program was a complete sham, and Austin was actually using the money to fund his lifestyle and pay off earlier investors.

Austin began by hosting free seminars all over Florida where he made the promise that he had found a legal loophole that allowed him to eliminate any debt, including mortgages, credit cards, and car loans. He further claimed that his team of legal and financial experts was working on the debt elimination process, and that investors would receive their returns within months.

The promise of quickly and effortlessly eliminating debt naturally attracted many individuals, and they invested thousands of dollars in the program. Austin used the money to fund his expensive lifestyle, buying a yacht, a private jet, and luxurious cars, among other things. He also used the money to pay off earlier investors to make the program seem successful.

However, the Miracle Money Method was a complete fraud, and Austin had no legal or financial expertise. In reality, he was using the funds from new investors to pay off earlier investors, creating a Ponzi scheme. As the program grew, Austin became more aggressive in his tactics to recruit new investors, offering special deals and promising even higher returns.

Eventually, the scheme collapsed, and Austin was arrested and charged with multiple counts of fraud. Many people lost their life savings in the scheme, and the case became an example of the dangers of debt elimination scams.

The story of the Miracle Money Method demonstrates how easy it is for scammers to take advantage of vulnerable people who are struggling with debt. It's crucial to note that debt elimination takes hard work and time, and there are no shortcuts. It's also important to recognize the red flags of a debt elimination scheme, such as upfront fees, promises of quick and effortless debt elimination, and the claim of a secret or legal loophole. These are typically signs of a scam, and anyone who asks for money upfront is likely running a fraud.

In conclusion, the Miracle Money Method was a debt elimination scheme in the early 2000s that promised investors returns of up to 10 times their investment by using a secret method to eliminate their debts. Unfortunately, the program was a complete fraud, and the organizer, Brent Austin, was using the money to fund his lifestyle and pay off earlier investors. Anyone who is struggling with debt should be cautious of any program that promises quick and easy debt elimination or asks for money upfront. Seeking help from a legitimate debt relief program is the best way to become debt-free without falling victim to a scam.

The Female Empowerment Scheme

The "Women's Empowerment" scam was a Ponzi scheme that defrauded investors of more than $300 million. The scheme was run by Gina Champion-Cain, a prominent San Diego businesswoman and philanthropist, who promised investors high returns by investing in women-owned businesses.

Champion-Cain claimed that her company, ANI Development, was developing properties in San Diego and elsewhere that would be leased to women-owned businesses. She told investors that their money would be used to fund these projects, and promised returns of up to 18% annually.

However, it soon became clear that Champion-Cain was using the money to fund her own lavish lifestyle. She bought multiple luxury homes, took expensive vacations, and made large political donations. Meanwhile, investors were left with nothing.

The scheme began to unravel in 2018 when one of Champion-Cain's lenders discovered that she had forged documents to obtain a loan. The lender reported her to the FBI, who began investigating her business practices. In August 2019, Champion-Cain was arrested and charged with fraud.

Champion-Cain pleaded guilty to charges of securities fraud, conspiracy, and obstruction of justice. She was sentenced to 15 years in prison and ordered to pay restitution to her victims.

The "Women's Empowerment" scam was particularly egregious because it preyed on the desire of investors to support women-owned businesses. Champion-Cain claimed that her investments were a way to support women's empowerment, but in reality, she was only interested in enriching herself.

The scheme also highlights the dangers of Ponzi schemes. Ponzi schemes rely on a constant influx of new investors to pay returns to earlier investors. They are unsustainable and always collapse eventually, leaving investors with nothing.

Investors should be wary of any investment opportunity that promises high returns with little risk. They should always do their due diligence and research the company and the people behind it before investing any money.

In the case of the "Women's Empowerment" scam, there were warning signs that investors should have heeded. For example, Champion-Cain was not a registered broker or investment advisor, and her company was not registered with the Securities and Exchange Commission. She also promised returns that were significantly higher than the market average, which should have raised red flags.

The "Women's Empowerment" scam was a devastating Ponzi scheme that defrauded investors of more than $300 million. Champion-Cain used the promise of investing in women-owned businesses to lure investors, but in reality, she was only interested in enriching herself. This scheme highlights the dangers of Ponzi schemes and the importance of doing due diligence before investing any money.

Curious Con Artists

Frank Abagnale Jr.

Frank Abagnale Jr. is a former con artist who gained notoriety in the 1960s for his elaborate schemes to defraud people and businesses of millions of dollars. He posed as a pilot, doctor, and lawyer, among other professions, using his charm, wit, and intelligence to gain people's trust and manipulate them into giving him money.

Abagnale was born in New York in 1948 and grew up in a broken home. His parents divorced when he was 16, and he ran away from home, eventually landing in New York City. There, he began forging checks, which led to his first arrest when he was only 16 years old. He escaped from police custody and fled to other states, where he continued his fraudulent activities.

One of Abagnale's most notable cons was his impersonation of a Pan Am pilot. He was able to fool people into believing he was a pilot by dressing in a Pan Am uniform and creating a fake ID with a fake Pan Am employee number. He used this persona to fly around the world for free and even convinced people to pay him for plane tickets. He later claimed to have flown more than 1 million miles in this way.

Abagnale also posed as a doctor, using his knowledge of medical terminology and his ability to fake a convincing French accent to convince hospital staff that he was a resident. He worked as a pediatrician for nearly a year, during which time he never actually treated a patient.

In addition to his impersonations, Abagnale also forged checks and other financial documents, creating elaborate schemes to defraud banks and other businesses. He was eventually caught by the FBI in 1969, after four years on the run, and was sentenced to 12 years in prison.

While in prison, Abagnale began to reform his ways. He agreed to work with the FBI to help them catch other con artists and fraudsters, using his expertise to advise on how to identify and prevent fraud. After serving only five years of his sentence, he was released on the condition that he would work for the government as a consultant and not profit from his crimes.

Abagnale went on to become a respected authority on fraud prevention and security, advising businesses and government agencies on how to protect themselves against fraud. He has written several books on the subject, including "Catch Me If You Can," which was later adapted into a popular film starring Leonardo DiCaprio as Abagnale.

Today, Abagnale is considered one of the foremost experts on fraud and security, and his advice is sought after by businesses and government agencies around the world. He has received numerous awards and honors for his contributions to the field, including the Presidential Distinguished Service Award and the Frank Carrington Crime Prevention Award.

Despite his checkered past, Abagnale is now regarded as a reformed criminal who has made amends for his past misdeeds. He has used his experience to help others avoid falling victim to fraud and has become an inspiration to many people who have overcome adversity and turned their lives around.

Frank Abagnale Jr. is a fascinating figure who gained notoriety for his elaborate schemes to defraud people and businesses of millions of dollars in the 1960s. His story, which was portrayed in the film "Catch Me If You Can," has become the stuff of legend, and his expertise on fraud prevention and security is still sought after today. While he may have started out as a criminal, Abagnale's story is ultimately one of redemption, and he serves as an inspiration to anyone who has faced adversity and overcome it.

Victor Lustig

Victor Lustig was a notorious con man who made a name for himself in the early 20th century by using his charm, intelligence, and quick wit to swindle people out of large sums of money. He is best known for selling the Eiffel Tower to scrap metal dealers in 1925, a feat that has become one of the most famous cons in history.

Lustig was born in Austria-Hungary in 1890 and spent much of his early life traveling around Europe. He was a master of deception from a young age, using his smooth talk and cunning to trick people into giving him money. By the time he was in his twenties, he had established himself as a successful con artist, specializing in selling phony investment opportunities to wealthy businessmen.

In the early 1920s, Lustig moved to the United States, where he continued his life of crime. He became particularly adept at forging documents, using his skills to create fake stock certificates and bonds that he would then sell to unsuspecting investors. He also began targeting government officials, using his connections and charm to bribe them into giving him large sums of money.

But Lustig's most famous con came in 1925, when he traveled to Paris and decided to sell the Eiffel Tower. He posed as a government official and invited a group of scrap metal dealers to a secret meeting, where he explained that the tower was in danger of collapsing and needed to be sold for scrap. After convincing the dealers that he was legitimate, he took their money and disappeared, leaving them with worthless documents and a sense of disbelief at having been conned so easily.

Lustig's Eiffel Tower scam was one of the most audacious cons of all time, and it cemented his reputation as one of the world's greatest con artists. He continued to operate for many years, using his skills to evade the law and stay one step ahead of his pursuers. He was eventually caught and spent time in prison, but even there he managed to con his fellow inmates out of money and goods.

Lustig died in prison in 1947, but his legacy as a master con artist has endured to this day. He is remembered not just for his daring scams, but also for his intelligence, charm, and ability to manipulate people to his advantage. His story has been the subject of many books and films, and he remains a fascinating and enigmatic figure in the history of crime.

In many ways, Lustig was a product of his time. The early 20th century was a period of great social and economic upheaval, and people were willing to take risks in order to make a quick fortune. Lustig was able to exploit this desire for wealth and security, using his talents to convince people to part with their money without a second thought.

But Lustig was also unique in his approach to crime. He was not a violent criminal, nor was he motivated by a desire for power or revenge. Instead, he saw himself as an entrepreneur of sorts, using his skills to create and sell phony products to a gullible public. He was a master of psychology, understanding how people think and what motivates them, and he used this knowledge to his advantage.

In the end, Lustig's legacy is a cautionary tale about the dangers of greed and the allure of quick riches. He was a man who was able to charm his way into the hearts and wallets of countless victims, and he did so with a sense of style and panache that made him one of the most memorable con artists of all time. But his story is also a reminder that crime never pays in the long run, and that those who seek to enrich themselves at the expense of others will eventually be caught and brought to justice.

Maria Anna Mozart

Maria Anna Mozart, known as "Nannerl," was born in Salzburg, Austria in 1751, the oldest of the Mozart siblings. Her younger brother, Wolfgang, would go on to become one of the most famous composers in history, but during her lifetime, Nannerl was also a talented musician and performer in her own right.

Nannerl was trained in music by her father, Leopold Mozart, who recognized her talent at a young age. Together with Wolfgang, Nannerl performed throughout Europe as a child prodigy, showcasing her skills on the keyboard and the violin.

However, as she grew older, Nannerl's opportunities to perform became limited. In the 18th century, it was not considered appropriate for women to have professional careers in music, and Nannerl was expected to focus on marriage and family instead.

Despite this, Nannerl continued to compose and perform music in private, and even wrote several pieces for her brother to play. But she was unable to achieve the same level of success as Wolfgang, who was able to build a career as a composer and performer.

Frustrated by her limited opportunities, Nannerl began to pose as a performer and composer in her brother's name. She wrote letters to potential employers and publishers, signing them with Wolfgang's name and claiming that he had written the music she had composed.

In some cases, Nannerl was successful in securing commissions and performance opportunities in this way. But ultimately, she was unable to sustain the deception, and her career as a composer and performer never took off.

Nannerl's story is a fascinating example of the challenges faced by women in the arts during the 18th century. Despite her considerable talent and dedication to music, she was limited by societal expectations and the gender norms of the time.

It's also worth noting that Nannerl's story is not unique. Many women throughout history have faced similar obstacles in pursuing careers in the arts, and their contributions to music, literature, and other creative fields have often been overlooked or marginalized.

Today, there is a growing awareness of the need to recognize and celebrate the achievements of women in the arts, and to support the next generation of female artists and performers. Organizations like the Women's Philharmonic Advocacy are working to promote the music of women composers and performers, while initiatives like the Women's Prize for Fiction are highlighting the work of female writers.

Maria Anna Mozart, or Nannerl, was a talented musician and composer in her own right, but was limited by societal expectations and gender norms. Her decision to pose as her brother in order to gain opportunities in the music industry highlights the challenges faced by women in the arts throughout history, and the need to support and celebrate their achievements.

George C. Parker

George C. Parker was a notorious con artist who gained notoriety in the early 20th century for his audacious scams. Born in 1860, Parker grew up in New York City and became known for his smooth talking and persuasive personality. He quickly realized that he could use these skills to make money by selling things that he didn't actually own.

One of Parker's most famous scams involved selling the Brooklyn Bridge to unsuspecting buyers. He would approach wealthy tourists and tell them that the bridge was for sale, claiming that he had the authority to sell it on behalf of the city. He would often dress up in a fake uniform and carry forged documents to make his story seem more convincing.

Despite the obvious absurdity of the scheme, Parker was able to convince several people to buy the bridge from him. In some cases, he even sold it multiple times to different buyers. Of course, none of the buyers ever received any ownership rights to the bridge, and Parker simply pocketed the money and disappeared.

But Parker didn't stop at selling the Brooklyn Bridge. He also claimed to be selling other New York City landmarks, including the Statue of Liberty, Madison Square Garden, and even the Metropolitan Museum of Art. He used a variety of tactics to convince his victims to part with their money, including forging documents, impersonating city officials, and making elaborate pitches about the investment potential of these landmarks.

One of Parker's most audacious scams involved the sale of Grant's Tomb, the final resting place of Ulysses S. Grant. He claimed that the tomb was in disrepair and that it needed to be sold to a private investor who could restore it to its former glory. Parker even went so far as to create a fake organization called the Grant Monument

Association, which he used to convince potential buyers that he had the authority to sell the tomb.

Of course, Parker didn't actually own any of these landmarks, and he never had any intention of selling them to his victims. Instead, he simply used their gullibility and greed to line his own pockets. It's estimated that Parker made hundreds of thousands of dollars from his various scams, which would be worth millions of dollars in today's money.

Parker's scams eventually caught up with him, and he was arrested and convicted of fraud multiple times throughout his life. But he remained unrepentant, and even continued to try and sell the Brooklyn Bridge from his prison cell. He died in 1936, having left a legacy as one of the most notorious con artists in American history.

The story of George C. Parker serves as a cautionary tale about the dangers of greed and the importance of skepticism. Despite the obvious absurdity of his schemes, Parker was able to convince many people to part with their money by playing on their desire for wealth and status. His legacy reminds us that there will always be those who seek to profit by taking advantage of others, and that it's up to each of us to be vigilant and skeptical in our dealings with others.

George C. Parker was a legendary con artist who sold various New York City landmarks to unsuspecting buyers. His audacious scams, including the sale of the Brooklyn Bridge, demonstrate the power of persuasion and the dangers of greed. While Parker's legacy is one of deception and dishonesty, it also serves as a reminder of the importance of skepticism and critical thinking in our interactions with others.

The Fox Sisters

The Fox Sisters, consisting of Margaret, Kate, and Leah, were three siblings from a small town in upstate New York who rose to fame in the mid-1800s as spiritual mediums who claimed to communicate with the dead. Their supposed ability to talk to the spirits of the departed drew large audiences and made them celebrities in their time. However, their career was eventually exposed as a fraud, and they fell from grace.

The sisters began their career as mediums in 1848, when Margaret and Kate claimed to hear strange knocking sounds in their home. They convinced their parents that these sounds were messages from the spirit world and began holding public seances to communicate with the spirits. The sisters' fame spread quickly, and they soon became well-known figures in the burgeoning spiritualist movement of the time.

The Fox Sisters' success was based on the idea that they were able to communicate with the spirits of the dead, and they used a range of techniques to convince people that this was true. They would often hold seances in darkened rooms, where they claimed to hear voices, see visions, and feel the touch of spirits. They also used a variety of props, such as bells, musical instruments, and tables that moved on their own, to create the illusion of supernatural activity.

The sisters' popularity grew rapidly, and they were soon traveling across the country to hold seances for paying audiences. They became known for their ability to provide personal messages from the spirits of departed loved ones, which they claimed were conveyed to them by a spirit known as "Mr. Splitfoot."

However, cracks began to appear in the sisters' facade. In 1850, a skeptical investigator named E.W. Capron attended one of their seances and exposed their methods as a fraud. He showed that the knocking sounds could be produced by the sisters themselves, and that their messages from the dead were often based on information they had obtained beforehand from their clients.

Despite this, the Fox Sisters continued to enjoy success for several years, and their fame even spread to Europe, where they held seances for members of the aristocracy. However, their reputation suffered a major blow in 1888, when Margaret Fox publicly admitted that their abilities as mediums were a fraud.

In a series of interviews with the New York World newspaper, Margaret revealed that the sisters had used a variety of tricks and techniques to deceive their audiences. She described how they had produced the knocking sounds by cracking their toe joints, and how they had used hidden wires and magnets to move tables and other objects during seances.

The revelation of the sisters' deception caused a sensation, and they were widely criticized and ridiculed in the press. However, despite the damage to their reputation, they continued to perform as mediums for several more years.

The story of the Fox Sisters is a cautionary tale about the power of belief and the dangers of fraud. The sisters were able to build a successful career by exploiting people's fears and anxieties about death and the afterlife, and by convincing them that they had access to hidden knowledge and wisdom. However, their fraud eventually caught up with them, and they were exposed as charlatans who had preyed on the gullibility of their audiences.

Today, the Fox Sisters are remembered as a fascinating footnote in the history of spiritualism, and as a cautionary tale about the dangers of believing too easily in the supernatural. Their story serves as a reminder that even the most convincing claims of the paranormal should be subject to scrutiny and skepticism, and that we should always be on guard against those who seek to exploit our fears and vulnerabilities for their own gain.

Eduardo de Valfierno

Eduardo de Valfierno was a skilled con artist who managed to pull off one of the most daring art heists in history: the theft of the Mona Lisa. But unlike most thieves who would simply try to sell the stolen masterpiece on the black market, Valfierno had a different plan. He wanted to sell copies of the painting to wealthy collectors who believed they were purchasing the real thing.

Valfierno was born in Argentina in 1874 and later moved to France, where he worked as a forger and con artist. He was known for his charm and charisma, which he used to manipulate people and convince them to part with their money. He soon realized that the art world was a particularly lucrative target, and he began to hatch a plan to steal one of the most valuable paintings in the world: the Mona Lisa.

In 1911, Valfierno hired a handyman named Vincenzo Peruggia to steal the painting from the Louvre Museum in Paris. Peruggia managed to smuggle the painting out of the museum by hiding it under his coat, and he brought it to Valfierno, who paid him for his services and then had the painting hidden away in a secret location.

But Valfierno's plan was far from over. He knew that trying to sell the actual Mona Lisa would be nearly impossible, since it was too well-known and too hot to handle. Instead, he decided to have copies made of the painting, and then sell those copies to wealthy buyers who believed they were purchasing the real thing.

Valfierno hired a talented forger named Yves Chaudron to create the copies, and he gave him detailed instructions on how to make them look as authentic as possible. Chaudron spent months painstakingly replicating the painting, making sure that every brushstroke and detail was perfect.

Once the copies were finished, Valfierno began to approach wealthy buyers and offer to sell them the Mona Lisa. He used his charm and salesmanship to convince them that they were getting a once-in-a-lifetime opportunity to own one of the world's most famous paintings. He even provided them with fake documents and certificates of authenticity to make the sale seem more legitimate.

Amazingly, Valfierno managed to sell at least six copies of the painting to various buyers. One of the buyers was a wealthy Argentinian collector named Eduardo de la Barra, who paid Valfierno the equivalent of $800,000 for what he believed was the real Mona Lisa. Another buyer was a wealthy American businessman named Armand Hammer, who paid $250,000 for a copy of the painting.

Valfierno's scheme was only discovered after the real Mona Lisa was recovered in 1913 and Peruggia was arrested. When questioned by police, Peruggia claimed that he had stolen the painting on behalf of an anonymous buyer who wanted a copy of the painting made. This led investigators to Valfierno, who was eventually arrested and charged with fraud and theft.

Valfierno's trial was a sensation, as people around the world were fascinated by the audacity of his scheme. He was ultimately found guilty and sentenced to five years in prison, but he served only a fraction of that time before being released.

Despite the fact that he was a criminal, many people still admire Valfierno for his ingenuity and audacity. He managed to steal one of the most famous paintings in the world and sell multiple copies of it to wealthy buyers, all without getting caught until after the fact.

In the years since the theft of the Mona Lisa, there have been countless attempts to steal other valuable works of art, but none have been as successful as Valfierno's.

Rachel Dolezal

Rachel Dolezal is a former African American Studies professor and civil rights activist who gained national attention in 2015 for claiming to be a black woman, despite being born to white parents. Dolezal's story is one of identity deception and cultural appropriation that sparked a debate on race and identity politics.

Dolezal was born in Montana in 1977, to white parents who were of German and Czech descent. She grew up with adopted black siblings and has claimed that her parents physically abused her and her siblings. She attended college in Mississippi and later moved to Idaho, where she became involved in the civil rights movement.

In 2014, Dolezal was elected as the president of the Spokane, Washington chapter of the National Association for the Advancement of Colored People (NAACP). She also worked as a part-time African American Studies professor at Eastern Washington University. During her tenure at the NAACP, she was instrumental in organizing various protests and campaigns against police brutality and racial discrimination.

However, in June 2015, her story came under scrutiny after her parents revealed to the media that she was, in fact, white. Dolezal initially denied the allegations, claiming that she was black and that race was a social construct. However, as the evidence mounted, she eventually admitted that she was born to white parents, but maintained that she identified as black.

The controversy surrounding Dolezal's racial identity sparked a nationwide debate on race and identity politics. Some accused her of cultural appropriation and using her white privilege to claim blackness, while others defended her as a transracial person who had the right to identify with any race she chose.

Despite the controversy, Dolezal continued to defend her position and even wrote a book titled "In Full Color: Finding My Place in a Black and White World." However, the book was poorly received and criticized for perpetuating stereotypes and not addressing the issues surrounding her deception.

In the aftermath of the controversy, Dolezal resigned from her position at the NAACP and was also forced to resign from her teaching position at Eastern Washington University. She faced widespread backlash and ridicule from the public and was even the subject of a Netflix documentary titled "The Rachel Divide."

Dolezal's story raises important questions about race, identity, and cultural appropriation. While some argue that individuals have the right to identify with any race they choose, others argue that racial identity is not a matter of choice but a matter of one's ancestry and lived experiences.

Furthermore, Dolezal's actions also highlight the complex power dynamics at play in society, particularly in the realm of race relations. As a white woman who claimed to be black, Dolezal was able to occupy spaces and positions of power that were traditionally reserved for black individuals. This raises important questions about the intersection of race, power, and privilege in society.

Rachel Dolezal's story is one of identity deception and cultural appropriation that sparked a nationwide debate on race and identity politics. While some defended her right to identify with any race she chose, others criticized her for using her white privilege to claim blackness. Ultimately, her story highlights the complex and nuanced issues surrounding race and identity in contemporary society.

Frank Bourassa

Frank Bourassa is a name that became synonymous with counterfeit money in Canada and beyond. Bourassa was a successful counterfeiter who managed to print and distribute millions of dollars in fake currency. He became one of the most notorious counterfeiters in history, and his story has been the subject of numerous documentaries, books, and articles.

Bourassa was born in 1971 in Quebec, Canada. He grew up in a working-class family and struggled with poverty throughout his childhood. In the early 1990s, he began working in the printing industry and quickly became fascinated with the technical aspects of printing. He learned everything he could about the printing process, including how to use high-end printing equipment and create sophisticated designs.

In the late 1990s, Bourassa decided to put his printing skills to use by creating counterfeit money. He started small, printing a few hundred dollars at a time and gradually increasing the amount he produced. He was careful to make sure that his counterfeit money looked and felt like real money, and he used high-quality paper and ink to ensure that his fakes were as convincing as possible.

Bourassa's counterfeit operation eventually grew to include several people, including his girlfriend, sister, and a few close friends. They worked together to produce large quantities of fake money, which Bourassa would then distribute to criminal organizations and individuals across Canada and the United States. He was able to stay one step ahead of the authorities by constantly changing his printing techniques and using sophisticated security features, such as holograms and watermarks, in his counterfeit bills.

Bourassa's success as a counterfeiter eventually caught up with him. In 2004, he was arrested by the Royal Canadian Mounted Police

(RCMP) and charged with counterfeiting. His trial was a media sensation, and he was portrayed as a modern-day Robin Hood by some members of the public who admired his ability to outsmart the authorities.

Despite his initial notoriety, Bourassa was eventually convicted and sentenced to six and a half years in prison. He was also ordered to pay millions of dollars in restitution to the Canadian government and other victims of his counterfeiting operation.

After serving his sentence, Bourassa remained somewhat of a controversial figure in Canada. Some people saw him as a criminal mastermind who had committed a serious crime, while others admired him for his ability to beat the system and outsmart the authorities. He was also seen as a symbol of the economic inequalities and social issues that plagued many people in Canada, particularly in Quebec.

Bourassa's story has been the subject of numerous books, documentaries, and articles. Some of these portray him as a criminal genius who managed to pull off one of the biggest counterfeiting operations in history, while others see him as a tragic figure who was driven to a life of crime by circumstances beyond his control.

Bourassa's story is a cautionary tale about the dangers of counterfeiting and the high price that criminals must pay for their actions. Although he was able to print millions of dollars in fake money, he ultimately paid a heavy price for his crimes and spent years of his life in prison. His story serves as a reminder that crime does not pay, and that the only way to achieve success is through hard work, honesty, and integrity.

Anna Sorokin

Anna Sorokin gained notoriety as a con artist who posed as a wealthy German heiress and swindled several businesses and individuals out of hundreds of thousands of dollars. Born in Russia in 1991, Sorokin moved to Germany with her family in 2007 before relocating to New York City in 2013.

In New York, Sorokin began living the high life, frequenting luxury hotels, private jets, and expensive restaurants, all while claiming to be a wealthy German heiress named Anna Delvey. She began networking in New York's social scene and building relationships with wealthy individuals, often promising them investments in her supposed art foundation.

Sorokin's web of lies began to unravel in 2017 when she attempted to secure a $22 million loan to fund her own private arts club. The loan was denied, and Sorokin was subsequently arrested in 2018 on multiple charges of grand larceny and theft of services.

At her trial in 2019, prosecutors painted Sorokin as a master manipulator who had no qualms about deceiving those around her. They presented evidence of Sorokin defrauding a luxury hotel out of thousands of dollars, using a bad check to pay for a lavish trip to Morocco, and even faking a bank statement to secure a $100,000 loan.

During the trial, Sorokin also came under scrutiny for her courtroom antics. She often appeared in designer clothes and appeared unfazed by the gravity of the charges against her. In one instance, she even dismissed her defense lawyer mid-trial and represented herself, claiming that she was being poorly represented.

Despite her attempts to defend herself, Sorokin was found guilty on multiple charges and sentenced to four to 12 years in prison. She was also ordered to pay nearly $200,000 in restitution and fines.

The Anna Sorokin case garnered significant media attention and sparked conversations about wealth, privilege, and the ease with which someone can pose as a wealthy socialite in New York City. Many were shocked by the audacity of Sorokin's actions and the extent to which she was able to deceive those around her.

Some also criticized the media's fascination with Sorokin, arguing that it perpetuated the same culture of privilege and excess that allowed her to thrive in the first place. Others pointed out that Sorokin was not the first person to pose as a wealthy heiress, citing the case of Gigi Jordan, a woman who posed as a billionaire to gain access to New York's elite social circles and was later convicted of murder.

Despite the controversy surrounding her case, the Anna Sorokin story remains a cautionary tale about the dangers of unchecked privilege and the ease with which someone can exploit the trust of those around them. Sorokin's case also serves as a reminder of the importance of due diligence and the need to verify the claims of those with whom we do business.

In the end, Sorokin's legacy will likely be that of a talented grifter who managed to deceive those around her with her charm and quick wit. Her story will undoubtedly be retold for years to come as a reminder of the power of deception and the dangers of unchecked privilege.

Elizabeth Holmes

Elizabeth Holmes is an American entrepreneur and founder of the now-defunct healthcare technology startup, Theranos. Born in 1984 in Washington, D.C., Holmes attended Stanford University but dropped out in her second year to pursue her business idea.

Holmes founded Theranos in 2003 at the age of 19, with the aim of revolutionizing the blood-testing industry. The company claimed to have developed a device that could perform a wide range of medical tests on a single drop of blood, which would make testing faster, cheaper, and more convenient for patients.

Theranos quickly attracted investors and partners, with Holmes becoming one of the youngest self-made female billionaires in the world. She also gained media attention for her personal style, which often included black turtlenecks, emulating Steve Jobs.

However, in 2015, investigative journalist John Carreyrou published an article in The Wall Street Journal, which raised doubts about the accuracy of Theranos' technology. Subsequent investigations by regulators and journalists revealed that the company had made false claims about its technology, misled investors and the public, and even endangered patients' lives.

The alleged fraud involved using commercially available blood testing machines and diluting the samples to get accurate results. Theranos' technology was never actually used in any patient tests, despite claims that it was being used in labs across the country.

Holmes and her former partner and COO, Sunny Balwani, were indicted in June 2018 on charges of wire fraud and conspiracy to commit wire fraud. They were accused of deceiving investors, doctors, and patients, as well as endangering patients' lives by providing inaccurate test results. Holmes was stripped of her billionaire status and resigned as CEO of Theranos in 2018.

Holmes and Balwani's trial began in August 2021, with prosecutors accusing them of lying about Theranos' technology, making false statements to investors, and defrauding doctors and patients. Holmes' defense argued that she was a well-intentioned but inexperienced entrepreneur who believed in her vision of transforming healthcare.

The trial concluded in December 2021, with Holmes being found guilty on four counts of fraud and conspiracy. She faces up to 20 years in prison for each count, with her sentencing scheduled for 2022.

The case of Elizabeth Holmes and Theranos has been described as one of the biggest corporate frauds in Silicon Valley history. The company's downfall has raised questions about the ethics of the tech industry, the need for more regulation, and the cult of personality that surrounds some of its most prominent figures.

Holmes' case also highlights the importance of accountability and transparency in business, particularly when it comes to dealing with people's health and wellbeing. The false promises made by Theranos and its founder have had real-world consequences for patients who relied on inaccurate test results.

The story of Elizabeth Holmes and Theranos has been the subject of numerous documentaries, podcasts, and books. The HBO documentary, "The Inventor: Out for Blood in Silicon Valley," and the book, "Bad Blood: Secrets and Lies in a Silicon Valley Startup" by John Carreyrou, provide in-depth accounts of the scandal and the people involved.

In conclusion, Elizabeth Holmes was a young and ambitious entrepreneur who aimed to revolutionize the healthcare industry with her blood-testing startup, Theranos. However, her ambition turned into deception as she and her partner allegedly defrauded investors, doctors, and patients with false claims about their technology.

Quirky Cybercriminals

The World's Most Famous Hacker

Kevin Mitnick, born in 1963, is a former computer hacker who gained notoriety in the 1990s for his exploits in hacking into computer systems and stealing confidential information. Mitnick's hacking career began in the 1980s, and he quickly became known for his skill in social engineering, a technique of manipulating people to divulge confidential information.

Mitnick's first significant hack occurred in 1981, when he hacked into the computer system of the Digital Equipment Corporation (DEC) to obtain their software source code. He continued to hack into computer systems, including those of major companies such as IBM, Motorola, and Sun Microsystems.

In 1995, Mitnick was arrested by the FBI after a two-year manhunt. He was charged with several computer-related crimes, including wire fraud and computer fraud. Mitnick spent nearly five years in prison, including eight months in solitary confinement, before he was released in 2000.

After his release from prison, Mitnick turned his attention to computer security and became a consultant for businesses and governments around the world. He has written several books about computer security, including "The Art of Deception" and "Ghost in the Wires," which detail his exploits as a hacker and his experiences in prison.

Mitnick's hacking career is notable for his use of social engineering techniques to gain access to computer systems. He often posed as someone with authority or credibility, such as a system administrator or a law enforcement officer, to persuade others to divulge confidential information. Mitnick also used his knowledge of computer systems to exploit vulnerabilities in security systems and gain access to confidential data.

Despite his criminal past, Mitnick is now regarded as a leading expert in computer security and is frequently called upon to speak at conferences and events around the world. He has also founded his own computer security consulting firm, Mitnick Security Consulting LLC, which provides services to businesses and governments.

Mitnick's case is significant because it highlights the dangers of social engineering and the importance of strong security protocols to prevent unauthorized access to confidential information. His case also helped to raise awareness of the need for stronger cybersecurity measures and the risks posed by cybercriminals.

In recent years, Mitnick has become an advocate for cybersecurity education and awareness, particularly among young people. He has spoken at numerous conferences and events to raise awareness of the risks posed by cybercriminals and the importance of protecting personal and confidential information.

In conclusion, Kevin Mitnick is a former computer hacker who gained notoriety for his exploits in hacking into computer systems and stealing confidential information. He is now a leading expert in computer security and is frequently called upon to speak at conferences and events around the world. Mitnick's case highlights the importance of strong security protocols and cybersecurity education to prevent unauthorized access to confidential information.

segvec

Albert Gonzalez, also known as "segvec," was a notorious cybercriminal who led one of the biggest credit card fraud schemes in history. Born in Cuba and raised in Miami, Gonzalez showed an early interest in computers and hacking, eventually dropping out of high school to pursue his criminal activities full-time.

Gonzalez first came to the attention of law enforcement in 2003, when he was arrested for hacking into the computer network of a major restaurant chain. He was released on bail and continued his hacking activities, eventually becoming the leader of a group of hackers who specialized in stealing credit and debit card numbers.

Gonzalez and his team used a variety of techniques to gain access to the computer systems of their targets. They used SQL injection attacks to exploit vulnerabilities in websites and malware to infect computers with keyloggers and other tools that allowed them to capture user credentials and other sensitive information.

One of Gonzalez's most audacious hacks was the one he carried out against TJX Companies, the parent company of retailers such as T.J. Maxx and Marshalls. Between 2005 and 2007, Gonzalez and his team hacked into TJX's computer systems and stole over 45 million credit and debit card numbers, making it the largest data breach at the time.

Gonzalez also targeted other major retailers such as Barnes & Noble, Sports Authority, and OfficeMax, as well as payment processors such as Heartland Payment Systems, from which he stole another 130 million credit and debit card numbers.

Gonzalez's criminal activities came to an end in 2008, when he was arrested by the U.S. Secret Service in Miami. He was eventually sentenced to 20 years in prison for his role in the TJX and Heartland breaches, as well as other cybercrimes.

Despite his notoriety as a cybercriminal, Gonzalez was also known for his extravagant lifestyle. He spent his ill-gotten gains on luxury cars, expensive watches, and high-end hotels and restaurants, often traveling to Europe and Asia on lavish vacations.

In addition to his prison sentence, Gonzalez was also ordered to pay millions of dollars in restitution to his victims. His case is considered a watershed moment in the history of cybercrime, as it highlighted the need for stronger cybersecurity measures to protect against the growing threat of data breaches and other cyberattacks.

Gonzalez's story is also a cautionary tale about the dangers of using technology for criminal purposes. Despite his early promise as a hacker, his greed and desire for wealth ultimately led to his downfall, serving as a warning to others who may be tempted to engage in cybercrime.

Albert Gonzalez was one of the most notorious cybercriminals of his time, responsible for some of the largest data breaches in history. While his exploits were impressive in their scope and scale, they also demonstrated the serious risks posed by cybercrime and the need for stronger security measures to protect against it. Gonzalez's legacy serves as a reminder of the importance of ethical behavior in the digital age, and the consequences that can result from using technology for criminal purposes.

The Silk Road

Ross Ulbricht was a young man with a passion for technology and libertarian ideals, who created the Silk Road, an online marketplace for illegal goods and services. Ulbricht saw the Silk Road as a way to enable free trade and individual liberty, unencumbered by government intervention. However, the FBI saw it as a criminal enterprise, and Ulbricht was eventually arrested and sentenced to life in prison.

Born in Austin, Texas in 1984, Ulbricht grew up in a supportive and loving family. His father was a physicist, and his mother was a trained nurse. Ulbricht showed an early interest in computers and coding, and by his early twenties, he had become involved in the world of libertarian activism. He was particularly interested in the concept of anarcho-capitalism, which advocates for the abolition of government intervention in the economy and other areas of life.

In 2011, Ulbricht began working on the Silk Road, an online marketplace that would allow people to buy and sell goods and services anonymously, using the digital currency Bitcoin. The Silk Road quickly became a hub for illegal drugs, fake IDs, and other contraband. Ulbricht used the pseudonym "Dread Pirate Roberts" to maintain his anonymity and to communicate with his customers and employees.

At its height, the Silk Road was generating millions of dollars in revenue each month. Ulbricht became known as a visionary entrepreneur and a hero to some in the libertarian community. However, the FBI saw the Silk Road as a major threat to public safety, and began investigating the site in 2012.

In October 2013, the FBI arrested Ulbricht in San Francisco and charged him with a range of offenses, including drug trafficking, money laundering, and computer hacking. The trial attracted significant media attention, with many people divided over whether Ulbricht was a criminal or a hero. Ulbricht's defense team argued that he was not "Dread Pirate Roberts" and that he had been set up as a fall guy by the real operator of the Silk Road. However, the evidence against Ulbricht was strong, and in May 2015, he was found guilty on all charges.

At his sentencing hearing, Ulbricht spoke about his regret for creating the Silk Road and the harm it had caused. However, the judge handed down a sentence of life in prison without the possibility of parole, stating that Ulbricht had "victimized thousands of people" and that his actions had caused "unprecedented" harm.

The Silk Road and the story of Ross Ulbricht have become legendary in the world of technology and criminal justice. Some see Ulbricht as a martyr for the cause of individual liberty and freedom, while others view him as a dangerous criminal who sought to profit from the misery of others. Regardless of one's perspective, the story of the Silk Road and its founder is a cautionary tale about the potential consequences of unchecked power and the dangers of the dark corners of the internet.

Ross Ulbricht was a brilliant and idealistic young man who became embroiled in a criminal enterprise that ultimately destroyed his life. His story is a reminder of the power of technology to enable both positive change and negative consequences, and the importance of responsible innovation and ethical decision-making. As the internet continues to evolve and shape our world, it is crucial that we remain vigilant against the dangers of cybercrime and the potential for harm to individuals and society as a whole.

Solo

Gary McKinnon (aka solo) is a British hacker who made headlines in the early 2000s for breaking into several high-profile U.S. government computer systems, including those of NASA, the Pentagon, and the U.S. Army. While some hackers are motivated by financial gain or political motives, McKinnon's motives were a bit different: he was searching for evidence of extraterrestrial life.

McKinnon, who was born in Glasgow in 1966, had a longstanding interest in UFOs and conspiracy theories. In the late 1990s, he began using his computer skills to search for evidence of government cover-ups related to extraterrestrial life. In 2001 and 2002, he hacked into the computer systems of several U.S. government agencies, including the Army, Navy, Air Force, Department of Defense, and NASA.

McKinnon's initial motivation for hacking was to find evidence of UFO cover-ups, but as he gained access to more and more sensitive government systems, he began to explore other areas as well. He claims to have discovered evidence of a secret space program, as well as evidence of government involvement in the 9/11 attacks.

Despite his claims, McKinnon's hacking activities were illegal and he was eventually caught. In 2002, U.S. authorities became aware of his activities and launched an investigation. McKinnon was arrested in 2005, and the U.S. government began extradition proceedings to bring him to the United States to face charges.

McKinnon's case quickly became a cause célèbre among UFO enthusiasts and free speech advocates, who argued that he was being persecuted for his beliefs rather than his actions. The British government initially refused to extradite him, citing concerns that he could face the death penalty if convicted. However, in 2012, the government reversed its decision and authorized his extradition.

McKinnon fought his extradition through the British courts, arguing that he could face torture or inhumane treatment if sent to the United States. However, in 2012, the European Court of Human Rights rejected his appeal, clearing the way for his extradition.

In the end, McKinnon struck a plea deal with U.S. authorities. He agreed to plead guilty to several charges related to computer hacking, and in exchange, prosecutors agreed to recommend that he be sentenced to no more than 63 months in prison. McKinnon was sentenced in 2013, and he served his sentence in the United Kingdom rather than being extradited to the United States.

McKinnon's case has been the subject of considerable controversy. Some argue that he was unfairly persecuted for his beliefs, while others point out that his hacking activities were illegal and had the potential to cause significant harm. Regardless of one's perspective, it is clear that McKinnon's case underscores the complex legal and ethical issues surrounding computer hacking and the search for extraterrestrial life.

In the years since his arrest and sentencing, McKinnon has largely stayed out of the public eye. However, his case continues to be cited as an example of the potential dangers of computer hacking and the need for strong cybersecurity measures to protect sensitive government systems.

Gary McKinnon's case is a fascinating and unusual example of a cybercriminal motivated by a unique set of beliefs and interests. While his hacking activities were illegal, they were driven by a quest for knowledge and a desire to uncover what he believed to be hidden truths. His case serves as a reminder of the potential consequences of unauthorized access to sensitive government systems and the importance of protecting against cyber attacks.

BadB

Vladislav Horohorin, also known as "BadB," was a Ukrainian hacker who operated in the late 2000s and early 2010s. He was one of the most successful cybercriminals of his time, known for stealing millions of dollars from American and European banks.

Horohorin's criminal activities began in his early twenties when he started hacking into bank and credit card databases. He was part of an underground community of cybercriminals who traded stolen credit card information on the dark web. Horohorin became one of the most prominent members of this community and built a reputation for being a skilled hacker.

Horohorin's activities came to the attention of law enforcement in the United States in 2009 when the Secret Service began investigating a group of cybercriminals who were stealing credit card information from American banks. The investigation led to the discovery of a website called "CarderPlanet," which was run by Horohorin. The website was a marketplace where cybercriminals could buy and sell stolen credit card information.

The Secret Service worked with law enforcement agencies in Ukraine and Israel to track down Horohorin. In 2010, he was arrested in France while on vacation. The French police discovered that Horohorin had been using a fake passport to travel around Europe. He was extradited to the United States to face charges of conspiracy, access device fraud, and aggravated identity theft.

Horohorin pleaded guilty to the charges and was sentenced to 88 months in prison in 2013. He was also ordered to pay $125 million in restitution to the victims of his crimes. In his plea agreement, Horohorin admitted to selling more than 1.8 million stolen credit card numbers on CarderPlanet, making more than $2.8 million in profits.

Horohorin's case was significant because it demonstrated the growing international nature of cybercrime. Horohorin was a Ukrainian citizen who operated from Russia and France, but his victims were mostly in the United States and Europe. The case also highlighted the difficulty of prosecuting cybercriminals, as they often operate across multiple jurisdictions and can easily conceal their identities.

Horohorin's case also showed the importance of international cooperation in fighting cybercrime. The Secret Service worked with law enforcement agencies in several countries to track down and arrest Horohorin, demonstrating the need for a coordinated effort to combat cybercrime.

After serving his sentence, Horohorin was deported to Ukraine in 2018. His case remains one of the most notable examples of a cybercriminal who operated on a global scale, and the significant impact that cybercrime can have on individuals and financial institutions.

Vladislav Horohorin, or "BadB," was a Ukrainian hacker who made millions of dollars by selling stolen credit card information on the dark web. He was one of the most successful cybercriminals of his time, and his case highlighted the international nature of cybercrime and the challenges involved in prosecuting cybercriminals. While Horohorin was ultimately caught and punished for his crimes, his case serves as a warning of the ongoing threat posed by cybercrime to individuals and financial institutions around the world.

The Russian

Dmitry Sklyarov is a Russian computer programmer who gained notoriety for his involvement in a controversial case involving digital rights management (DRM) and the DMCA (Digital Millennium Copyright Act). His case raised important questions about the role of technology in the digital age and the limits of copyright law.

Born in Moscow in 1972, Sklyarov studied mathematics and computer science at Moscow State University. After completing his studies, he worked for a Russian software company called Elcomsoft, which specialized in developing password recovery tools for encrypted files. In 2000, Sklyarov began working on a program that could remove DRM protections from Adobe e-books.

At the time, Adobe's e-books were protected by a technology called "e-book exchange" (EBX), which prevented users from copying, printing, or sharing e-books without permission. Sklyarov's program, known as the Advanced eBook Processor (AEBPR), allowed users to remove the EBX protection and convert Adobe e-books into other formats.

In July 2001, Sklyarov presented his findings at the DEF CON hacking conference in Las Vegas. His presentation generated a great deal of interest and controversy, as many people saw the EBX protections as overly restrictive and an infringement on their rights as consumers.

However, Sklyarov's actions caught the attention of the U.S. government, which charged him and his employer, Elcomsoft, with violating the DMCA. The DMCA criminalized the production and distribution of software that circumvented digital rights management protections, even if the software was designed for legitimate purposes.

Sklyarov was arrested by the FBI and charged with five counts of violating the DMCA. He was held in jail for five days before being released on bail. Sklyarov's arrest sparked outrage in the tech community, which saw it as a violation of free speech and an attempt to stifle innovation.

The case went to trial in December 2002, with Sklyarov facing a possible sentence of up to 25 years in prison and a $2.25 million fine. However, Sklyarov agreed to a plea bargain in which he pleaded guilty to a single count of trafficking in circumvention devices. He was sentenced to three years of probation and was prohibited from working on any projects related to digital rights management.

The Sklyarov case raised important questions about the role of copyright law in the digital age and the limits of technological innovation. Many critics saw the DMCA as overly broad and restrictive, and argued that it stifled innovation and creativity by limiting the ability of researchers and programmers to explore new technologies and methods.

The case also highlighted the importance of cybersecurity and the need for stronger protections against cybercrime. Sklyarov's actions showed how vulnerable digital content was to hacking and theft, and underscored the importance of robust security measures to protect against such threats.

After his release, Sklyarov returned to Russia, where he continued to work in the software industry. He also became an advocate for digital rights and internet freedom, and has spoken out against the DMCA and other restrictive copyright laws.

Dmitry Sklyarov's case brought attention to the need for balance between the interests of copyright owners and the freedom of speech and innovation. While his actions were deemed illegal under the DMCA, many argue that the law is too restrictive and stifles innovation

The Hacktivist

Jeremy Hammond is an American hacktivist who gained notoriety for his involvement in various cyberattacks against high-profile targets. Born in Chicago in 1985, Hammond became interested in computer hacking at a young age and began participating in online communities focused on activism and hacktivism.

In 2011, Hammond was arrested for his involvement in the breach of the security firm Stratfor, which resulted in the theft of thousands of confidential documents and the exposure of sensitive information about the company's clients. The attack was carried out by the hacktivist collective Anonymous and its offshoot, LulzSec, with Hammond playing a key role in the operation.

Following his arrest, Hammond was charged with multiple counts of computer fraud and conspiracy, and faced up to 10 years in prison. He pleaded guilty to one count of conspiracy and was sentenced to the maximum term of 10 years in November 2013.

Hammond's case sparked controversy among supporters of hacktivism and free speech, who saw his prosecution as a heavy-handed response to online activism. Some argued that his actions were motivated by a desire to expose corporate and government wrongdoing, and that he should be viewed as a whistleblower rather than a criminal.

During his time in prison, Hammond continued to be an outspoken critic of government surveillance and corporate influence on politics. He also maintained a blog and wrote articles for various publications, including The Guardian and Rolling Stone.

In 2015, Hammond was transferred to a halfway house in Chicago as part of a reduction in his sentence. However, his release was short-lived, as he was re-arrested in April of that year for violating the terms of his supervised release by using a computer without permission.

In 2019, Hammond was released from prison after serving seven years of his 10-year sentence. Upon his release, he continued to be an active participant in the hacktivist community, speaking at events and advocating for free speech and government transparency.

While Hammond's actions were controversial and led to his imprisonment, they also brought attention to the issue of government and corporate surveillance, as well as the role of hacktivism in modern activism. His case serves as a reminder of the ongoing tension between those who see hacking as a tool for exposing wrongdoing and those who view it as a criminal act.

McAfee

John McAfee was a computer programmer and entrepreneur who founded the McAfee antivirus software company in 1987. However, he became infamous not only for his contributions to the technology industry but also for his involvement in various controversies and cybercrimes.

Born in the United Kingdom in 1945, McAfee grew up in the United States and graduated from Roanoke College with a degree in mathematics in 1967. He started his career as a programmer and worked for various technology companies before founding McAfee Associates in 1987.

McAfee Associates developed and marketed antivirus software for personal computers, which became popular as the use of computers grew in the 1990s. McAfee became a billionaire after the company went public in 1992, but he resigned as CEO in 1994 due to personal issues.

After leaving McAfee Associates, John McAfee became involved in various controversies and legal troubles. In 2010, he was arrested in Belize on suspicion of manufacturing methamphetamine and possession of unlicensed weapons. He was released without charge but continued to live in Belize until 2012, when he fled the country after being sought for questioning in connection with the murder of his neighbor.

McAfee's involvement in cybercrimes began to surface in the early 2000s. In 2008, he was sued by Intel, which had acquired McAfee Associates in 2010, for using his name in a business venture without permission. The lawsuit was settled in 2009, and McAfee was allowed to continue using his name for commercial purposes.

In 2012, McAfee was implicated in a murder investigation in Belize. He claimed that he was being framed by the government and went into hiding, leading to a highly publicized manhunt. McAfee was eventually arrested in Guatemala for entering the country illegally and was deported to the United States.

After returning to the U.S., McAfee became involved in promoting various controversial products and services, including herbal supplements and privacy software. He also became interested in cryptocurrencies and was a vocal advocate for the use of bitcoin.

McAfee was also accused of promoting fraudulent cryptocurrency schemes. In 2018, he was sued by the U.S. Securities and Exchange Commission for promoting initial coin offerings (ICOs) without disclosing that he was being paid to do so. The lawsuit claimed that McAfee made over $23 million in undisclosed compensation from promoting ICOs.

McAfee was also known for his involvement in the "Lavabit" case, in which the secure email service Lavabit shut down in 2013 after being forced by the U.S. government to hand over its SSL keys. McAfee offered to help Lavabit's founder, Ladar Levison, by providing him with a secure email service that could not be accessed by the government. However, the project never came to fruition.

In 2019, John McAfee was indicted for tax evasion by the U.S. Department of Justice. He was accused of failing to file tax returns from 2014 to 2018 and hiding assets, including a yacht and real estate, from the government. McAfee was arrested in Spain in October 2020 at the request of the U.S. government, but he was found dead in his jail cell in June 2021, in what was ruled a suicide.

Seleznev

Roman Seleznev was a Russian cybercriminal who was sentenced to 27 years in prison by a U.S. court in 2016 for his role in one of the largest data breaches in U.S. history. Seleznev was responsible for hacking into point-of-sale systems at more than 200 businesses across the U.S. and stealing credit card information from millions of customers.

Born in Vladivostok, Russia, in 1984, Seleznev was the son of a prominent Russian politician, Valery Seleznev. He started hacking at a young age and became involved in various cybercriminal activities, including selling stolen credit card information on online forums.

In 2009, Seleznev started focusing on point-of-sale systems, which are used by businesses to process credit card payments. He developed and used malware known as "Carder's Paradise" to infiltrate the systems and steal credit card information. He would then sell the information on underground forums or use it to make fraudulent purchases.

Seleznev's targets included restaurants, bars, and other small businesses across the U.S. He used various aliases and fake identities to cover his tracks, and he was known for his ability to evade law enforcement agencies.

Seleznev's activities came to light in 2011, when federal authorities in the U.S. launched an investigation into a data breach at a restaurant chain in the Pacific Northwest. They traced the breach back to Seleznev and discovered that he was responsible for similar attacks at other businesses across the country.

In 2014, Seleznev was arrested in the Maldives, where he was on vacation. He was then extradited to the U.S. to face charges of hacking, wire fraud, and identity theft.

During his trial in the U.S., Seleznev's defense team argued that he was a victim of the U.S. government's overreach and that he was illegally arrested in the Maldives. They also argued that the evidence against Seleznev was obtained illegally and that his rights had been violated.

However, the prosecution presented evidence showing that Seleznev had made millions of dollars from his cybercriminal activities and that he had used his father's political connections to evade arrest for years.

In 2016, Seleznev was found guilty on 38 counts, including hacking, wire fraud, and identity theft. He was sentenced to 27 years in prison and ordered to pay $170 million in restitution to his victims.

The case against Seleznev was notable for its use of the Computer Fraud and Abuse Act, a controversial law that has been criticized for its broad definition of hacking and its potential to criminalize minor computer-related activities. Seleznev's defense team argued that the law was unconstitutional and that it was used to unfairly target him.

Seleznev's case also highlighted the growing problem of cybercrime and the need for stronger cybersecurity measures. The use of point-of-sale malware has become increasingly common in recent years, and businesses of all sizes are vulnerable to these attacks.

In the aftermath of Seleznev's arrest and conviction, law enforcement agencies around the world have stepped up their efforts to combat cybercrime. The case also serves as a warning to cybercriminals that they will be held accountable for their actions, no matter where in the world they operate from.

Iceman

Max Butler, also known as "Iceman," was a former cybersecurity expert turned cybercriminal who orchestrated one of the most significant data breaches in history. His exploits and subsequent arrest in 2007 shed light on the growing problem of cybercrime and demonstrated the need for stronger cybersecurity measures.

Butler's early life is relatively unknown, but he was born in 1976 and grew up in California. He became interested in computers at a young age and developed an interest in cybersecurity. Butler studied computer science at a community college but dropped out before completing his degree.

Despite lacking formal education, Butler quickly gained a reputation as a skilled hacker and cybersecurity expert. In the late 1990s, he founded a cybersecurity firm called Max Vision, which provided security consulting services to businesses and government agencies.

However, Butler's seemingly legitimate business was a front for his criminal activities. In 2002, he was arrested for hacking into the computer systems of a company he had been hired to protect. He was sentenced to 18 months in prison but was released after just six months for good behavior.

Following his release, Butler went underground and began to operate on the dark web, where he quickly gained a reputation as a prolific cybercriminal. He used a variety of hacking techniques, including SQL injection attacks, to gain access to sensitive data, including credit card numbers and personal information.

One of Butler's most significant exploits was the theft of more than 45 million credit card numbers from TJX Companies, the parent company of retailers including TJ Maxx and Marshalls. Butler and his team of hackers used a combination of social engineering and malware to access the company's payment processing systems and steal the credit card data.

Butler then sold the stolen credit card numbers on the dark web, making millions of dollars in the process. He used a variety of aliases and encrypted communication channels to avoid detection by law enforcement.

However, Butler's criminal activities eventually caught up with him. In 2007, he was arrested in San Francisco following a joint investigation by the Secret Service and the Department of Justice. He was charged with conspiracy, fraud, and identity theft, among other crimes.

Butler pleaded guilty to 19 counts and was sentenced to 13 years in prison in 2010. He cooperated with authorities and provided valuable information about other cybercriminals, which led to several other arrests and convictions.

Butler's case was significant because it highlighted the growing problem of cybercrime and demonstrated the need for stronger cybersecurity measures. It also showed that even the most skilled hackers and cybersecurity experts are not immune to prosecution.

After serving his sentence, Butler was deported to Belarus, where he reportedly resumed his criminal activities. He was arrested again in 2017 in Thailand for allegedly conspiring to commit money laundering and wire fraud.

End Note

The world of strange true crime is both fascinating and disturbing. The cases covered in this book, from unusual heists to peculiar Ponzi schemes, demonstrate the depth and variety of human behavior, and the many ways that people can break the law. While we may think we understand human behavior and the motives behind criminal activity, these tales show us that there are always new twists and turns to the human psyche.

The wide variety of crimes highlighted in this book demonstrate that there is no limit to the creativity and audacity of some criminals. From the daring bank robberies to the elaborate Ponzi schemes, the unusual methods used by these criminals show us that the only limit is one's own imagination.

However, while these stories may be intriguing and even entertaining in their strangeness, they also remind us of the real harm that these criminals inflicted upon their victims. The impact of their actions, whether it be financial ruin, emotional trauma, or loss of life, cannot be overlooked.

Moreover, these stories show us the importance of vigilance and caution in our daily lives. The crimes may seem outlandish, but they were all carried out by real people in the real world. We must remain aware of the dangers and take steps to protect ourselves and those around us.

In the end, the stories of strange true crime both fascinate and unsettle us. They challenge our assumptions about human behavior and remind us of the fragility of our safety and security. But ultimately, they also inspire us to be more vigilant, more cautious, and more aware of the world around us.

Printed in Great Britain
by Amazon